Stagecoach to Serenity

After Darren Norton shoots Arthur Hamlin dead during a card game, he goes on the run, leaving behind his girlfriend, Sal the Gal. A reward is put up for his capture and bounty hunter Gustavus Greeley is soon on his trail. He catches Norton in the hills and intends to take him back to Serenity by stagecoach to stand trial.

But there are several other passengers on the stage and the guard is new to the route. Greeley soon begins to wonder if one of them plans to help his prisoner escape. He faces a hard and dangerous journey, with death along the way, before he can bring Norton to justice.

Stagecoach to Serenity

Steven Gray

A Black Horse Western

ROBERT HALE

ISBN 978-0-7198-2676-4

The Crowood Press
The Stable Block
Crowood Lane
Ramsbury
Marlborough
Wiltshire SN8 2HR

www.bhwesterns.com

Robert Hale is an imprint
of The Crowood Press

Typeset by
Derek Doyle & Associates, Shaw Heath
Printed and bound in Great Britain by
CPI Group (UK) Ltd, Croydon, CR0 4YY

CHAPTER ONE

Bright lights, loud talk and the music of a honky-tonk piano spilled out from Serenity's Star Saloon. And when Darren Norton pushed open the batwing doors, his nose was assailed by the smells of cigarette smoke, whiskey and sweat.

Not that on a Wednesday night the saloon was crowded, but several cowboys lined the bar or stood around the piano player singing bawdy songs. A couple of girls – neither anywhere near as pretty as Sal the Gal but wearing dresses cut low enough to be interesting – worked the room. Best of all, a poker game was underway at a corner table. All four players were townsmen and would be easy to cheat. Norton didn't recognize three of them but, even better still, the fourth was Arthur Hamlin. He grinned. It would be a pleasure to take that young idiot's money from him. Again!

Another quick glance round showed that Marshal Rayner wasn't in evidence. Nor was his deputy, Frank Evans, the eager young lawman with whom he'd had several run-ins and who was just longing for any sort of excuse to throw him in jail.

Norton went up to the bar. 'Bottle of whiskey.'

'You got the money?' The bartender knew him of old.

'Sure.' Norton threw several coins on the bar.

'Honestly come by?'

'Yeah.' Well, come by anyway.

Norton poured himself a glass of the whiskey and after downing it in one go, rested his elbows on the bar and surveyed the poker players. Quickly he calculated how much money they were betting with and what the stakes were likely to be on each game. Not a fortune, but enough. He wasn't concerned about the three older men or even about the money, not really, but, boy, did he want to beat Arthur.

Arthur was the same age as him, twenty-five, and almost as tall. There the resemblance ended. Norton was broad-shouldered and his skin was tanned from spending most of the time outdoors. His hands were calloused. He had long and untidy black hair and was unshaven. He wore comfortable clothes and boots. And while he did odd jobs now and then, he mostly lived by his wits. Or his fists. Even his pistol on occasion.

Whereas Arthur was the respectable son of the respectable owner of the gun-shop. He looked like the townsman he was, with pallid skin and unblemished hands. Hell, he wore store-bought suits and shoes. And he was so boring he'd probably never done anything wrong in his whole life.

Almost from the day Norton rode into Serenity, the pair had made it plain neither could abide the other.

The gamblers finished their game. Clutching his glass

and the bottle, Norton sauntered over to the table. 'Room for another player?'

Arthur didn't look pleased but the other three, even though they were probably aware of Norton's reputation, didn't raise any objection. One of them got to his feet and gathering up the little money left in front of him, said, 'I'm out anyway. I ain't had a good night and I've lost too much as it is. I ain't losing any more. You can take my place, mister, and good luck to you.'

Luck, as far as Norton was concerned, rarely came into his game.

'We don't want any trouble, Darren,' Arthur said.

Norton spread his hands as if to say 'who me?'. 'Just wanna play poker is all. Here.' He poured out generous drinks for them all. 'I'm in funds at the moment.'

'That might change by the end of the evening,' the man opposite him said.

Norton laughed. No chance of that.

Arthur grimaced. 'Who did you rob to get so much money?'

'No one,' Norton said indignantly. 'Did some work for Old Man Henderson down at the livery. You can ask him iffen you don't believe me.'

Of course Arthur was right: he had also committed robbery. He'd fooled the lone traveller he'd helped with his horse into telling him where he was going once he left Serenity. Then he'd followed him, held him up and stolen his money. And beaten him so badly, with a warning he'd get more of the same if he showed his face in town again, that Norton knew the stranger wouldn't dare come back and report the theft to the marshal. Arthur didn't need to

7

know any of that.

'We goin' to play cards or not?' the other man said. 'Your deal, Arthur.'

Somewhat sulkily, Arthur shuffled the pack. Norton thought that if the young man had any sense he'd get up and walk away from the game. It was probably what he wanted to do, but pride wouldn't let him. He wouldn't want anyone wondering if he was afraid of Norton, especially Norton himself. Darren grinned. That suited him. This way he could get the better of the pompous bastard!

Norton deliberately lost a game here and there, just to make it look good. As he'd thought, the stakes weren't high but that was okay. Better to win small amounts steadily rather than such large pots that the other men would get worked up and suspicious or angry. No one would miss what they were losing, even though they lost nearly every hand.

He was aware of Arthur studying him more than he was studying his cards, trying to catch him out. That just made Arthur easier to beat.

At one point one of the girls came over and draped herself over Norton's shoulders, trying to attract his attention. He made it clear he wasn't interested. Naturally she didn't bother Arthur. Everyone knew Arthur was engaged to be married to a girl, Irene someone or the other, from a nearby ranch and that he, poor sap, remained faithful to her, whatever the temptation.

In his own way Norton was faithful to Sal the Gal; well, not exactly faithful but she'd always be his first choice, even though she was so damned expensive he couldn't often afford her. There would be hell to pay if she found out he sometimes resorted to cheaper girls and Norton hoped she never would; Sal's temper was best avoided. Luckily tonight with the way things were going, with no one suspecting a thing, once he left the saloon he'd have enough cash in his pocket to be able to go to Queenie's brothel and pay for a whole night with Sal. Boy, was he looking forward to that! Queenie might not like or approve of him, but she never turned down money.

Just one more game and he'd call it quits. It was then that everything that had been going right, went very, very wrong. Quite how Norton wasn't sure.

The amount he'd drunk might have had something to do with it, causing him to get cocky and careless. Maybe he was over-anxious to teach Arthur a lesson. Or maybe his mind was on Sal.

But. . . .

'Hey!' Arthur suddenly yelled. 'You cheat, Darren, I knew it! You cheated! I saw you.'

Taken by surprise, Norton stood up so abruptly his chair was knocked to the floor. For a moment the room seemed to whirl around him and he grabbed the edge of the table to steady himself.

'No I didn't,' he started to protest.

'You're not fooling me. You're holding four Queens.' Before Norton could stop him, Arthur got to his feet as well and reached out to turn over the five cards laying on the table. Sure enough, besides the two of spades there were the Queens of Hearts, Spades, Diamonds and Clubs. Arthur stared in triumph at Darren while the other two players began to get shocked and furious.

'I always knew you were a damn cheat, Darren, and now

I've caught you at it. Hey, barkeep, send for the marshal.'

While cheating at cards hardly warranted calling in the law, the bartender was only too happy to oblige. Norton had caused enough trouble at The Star in the past that it would be a pleasure to see him locked up or, better yet, run out of town, however flimsy the excuse. And Rayner, who was getting fed up with Darren's antics, would be only too happy to oblige.

Norton was aware that everything in the saloon had come to a halt, the place suddenly quiet and still. Most people hated cheats and everyone stared at him, holding their breath. He was caught fair and square.

He didn't waste time in protesting his innocence. Instead he lost his temper and his wits and, pulling his gun from its holster, shot Arthur between the eyes.

Arthur dropped to the floor, stone cold dead, look of triumph still on his face.

'You damn fool!' one of the other players shouted, while a girl screamed and the rest of the saloon's customers dived for whatever cover they could find.

'Marshal's on his way!'

'Get the bastard!'

'Don't try anything,' Norton warned. 'Or I'll shoot.'

'Watch out,' someone cried unnecessarily.

He was aware of dazed faces and scared, irate eyes accusing him.

With a shaky hand, he kept his gun trained on those nearest him. At the same time, he picked up as much money as he could from the table, stuffing coins and notes into his pockets. Fearing he'd wasted too much time already and that Marshal Rayner would be here before he

10

could escape, he swiftly backed to the doors and slid out into the cold night air.

Several horses waited outside, tied to the hitching post. Gulping for breath, heart pounding, with hands that shook violently, he somehow managed to untie the reins of the one nearest to him. He vaulted into the saddle. What did horse-theft matter when he'd just committed murder?

With yells and shots following him, he spurred away into the night. He was soon swallowed up by the darkness.

What had he done? Why? He couldn't believe what had happened. He had to blink away tears of remorse and fear.

Robbery at gunpoint was one thing, beating up his victim sometimes necessary, cheating at cards quite acceptable. But shooting a young man in cold blood – especially when that young man was well liked and well respected, in front of a dozen or more witnesses – was just about the stupidest and most senseless thing he'd ever done. Appalling too. He might not have liked Arthur, but that didn't mean he'd wanted to kill him.

Norton's only excuse was that while he was completely sober now, he'd been drunk and drink had made him furious and frightened. He'd reacted to the accusation without thought.

Now he must ride fast and ride far. Forget all about Sal the Gal. For now anyway. Surely he could outwit Marshal Rayner and whatever posse he might raise. He had money with him. He'd be okay. He must get away or face the hangman's noose for sure.

CHAPTER TWO

The posse lost Norton's trail where it came out of a dry creek-bed and promptly disappeared in the brush and scrub. Marshal Rayner and the men with him rode up and down the canyon floor in all directions and even up to the rim of the hill overlooking the canyon. They found no sign of the man they were chasing.

The hastily assembled posse had set out after Darren Norton at daybreak and had been out for almost three days now. Rayner had known it was always going to be difficult to catch him.

Although Frank Evans was a reasonably good tracker, Norton had had a long start on them. Not only that, but instead of riding for the desert where he, or at least his dust, would be easy to spot, he'd headed for the foothills. There whenever Evans found his trail it was quickly lost amongst the rocks and shale and streams. Now night was yet again almost here and by morning Norton could be miles away.

Rayner hated to admit defeat, but he could see no point

in going on.'We'll have to go back to Serenity,' he told the other men.

Most of them looked relieved; they had families and jobs waiting for them. But not so his deputy.

'We can't just let the bastard get away,' Evans objected. He was a determined and capable young man, who'd only recently been appointed as a deputy marshal. He was eager to uphold the law and he'd been a good friend of Arthur Hamlin's too. 'Not after what he did.' He raised eyes to the top of the ridge as if willing Norton to appear there so they could resume the chase.

'Believe me, Frank, I don't like it either.' Rayner sighed and pushed his hat to the back of his head, wiping sweat away from his forehead with his bandanna. 'But we're just chasing our tails. And all the while we stay out here it just gives the bastard more time to slip away and never be found.'

'Suppose you're right,' Evans nodded reluctantly. 'What are you goin' to do?'

'When we get back to town, I'll send messages out to the law in all the towns between here and the border and at every railroad halt – never mind the cost! – asking that a watch be kept out for him. And if it ain't been done already, I'll get the Town Council to put up some reward money for his capture so a Wanted Poster can be issued. He'll be caught before long, don't worry.'

'I hope so. I surely want to see the bastard hanged until he's good and dead.'

Rayner clapped his deputy on the back. 'Me too.'

Sal the Gal stood before the cheval mirror in her room at the brothel, admiring her reflection. Yes, she would do. So would the new black dress that was cut so tight and low it showed off her splendid figure, hinting what was underneath the silky material.

She was a beautiful girl of twenty-three with hair that hung in curls down to her waist, blue eyes, pale skin and an innocent face. And all that despite the fact she had been a prostitute since she fled home on her sixteenth birthday. That was the day her abusive father abused her once too often and she stopped him with a knife to his dark heart. Instead of giving thanks for his death, her mother screamed bloody murder and wept for the man who'd regularly beaten them both every Saturday night when he came home drunk from the saloon.

There and then Sal made up her mind she was never going to be anyone's victim ever again.

Growing up, she'd had little in the way of book learning and with no education her choice of career was limited. She could either work long hours in a shop or factory for little pay, at the mercy of yet more men, or as some kind of servant at the mercy of a woman. Or become a prostitute. OK, that involved men too but if she was clever enough it was also a way to earn a fortune, at their expense.

In order to survive, she'd always had to be calculating and shrewd and starting out on her chosen career was no different. She'd turned herself into a girl every man fantasized over and straight off she'd proved a success; partly because in the main she enjoyed what she did and mostly because, even when she didn't, she was still able to fool her clients into thinking they were special.

Now she felt she was experienced enough to run a

brothel of her own. To be the madam. Able to sit back and rake in the profits while other girls entertained the customers, although, for old times sake, she might entertain one or two favourites.

She'd liked Darren Norton from the first moment she saw him. He was good-looking and funny. She liked the way he looked at her with adoration in his eyes and, even more, how he loved her and how he did what she told him to. She liked his body and she even liked the fact that they could be friends as well as lovers, something she had never experienced before. A short while ago she'd suggested to him that they go into business together; his brawn and her looks and know-how would surely be a winning combination. They could move to San Francisco where there were fortunes just waiting to be made.

Naturally he'd agreed and left her to decide when the time was right. And then the idiot had gone and shot the Hamlin boy. All over a stupid game of poker.

Right now she was furious with him for letting her down.

The door opened and Queenie came in, without knocking of course. The madam was in her fifties, short, ugly and incredibly plump from all the chocolates she ate. She had a heart of stone and ruled the brothel with the help of a cane and the huge ruffian she employed to keep order.

Sal had worked for her since her arrival in Serenity a couple of years ago. At first, being two of a kind thinking only of themselves and how to exploit others, they had gotten along reasonably well. These days Sal was getting increasingly fed up with Queenie's high-handed manner and casual cruelty and at taking orders from her when she didn't need anyone telling her what to do. She was also sure that the madam regularly cheated her and the other girls out of some of what they earned.

She was ready to show Queenie that she was no longer prepared to be bossed around and treated badly. Unfortunately Queenie, with her long experience in the trade, knew exactly how Sal felt and was becoming more and more demanding and harsh, enjoying wielding what she saw as her power over the girl.

Unfortunately for Queenie, what she didn't know was that Sal was quite prepared to do anything – absolutely anything – to get her own way. She'd done so before; she would do so again.

'What are you doing still up here?' Queenie demanded in her shrill voice. 'Time to get your skinny ass down to the parlour. Men'll be coming by soon. Don't want to disappoint 'em, do you?'

'No,' Sal muttered. 'I'll be down in a minute.'

'You ain't, I'll take my cane to you.'

Queenie had never had cause to dare hurt Sal physically but the madam was longing for an excuse and the opportunity to show her who was boss. Woe betide Queenie if she tried!

'I said I'll be down.' Sal's hands clenched into tiny fists. How she longed to smash the smirk off the madam's face.

'See you are. Don't want you moping up here by yourself, just cos your boyfriend's gone. That ain't what I pay you for. I pay you to be nice.'

'Ain't I always?'

'Yeah,' Queenie chuckled crudely. 'I'll give you that.

You surely like what you do.' She paused in the doorway. 'By the way, the marshal and his posse came back a while earlier.' That was the real reason Queenie had come to her room, the reason for her smirk.

Sal did her best not to give the madam any satisfaction by showing her fear. Had they caught Darren? Was he in jail? 'Really?' She affected boredom.

'They was alone,' Queenie went on. 'Yeah, missy, thought that'd please you. Seems your boyfriend got away from 'em. Not that that's a surprise seeing as how stupid old Rayner was in charge.'

Knowing Rayner wasn't that stupid or that old, it took all Sal's strength of mind not to show how relieved she was, which would only make Queenie laugh.

'Trouble is he also got away from you. He's left you in the lurch.' Queenie grinned when Sal didn't say anything. 'Always said he was a no-good sonofabitch. See how much better off you are staying here with me and not running off with him somewhere else to start your own place.'

Had Queenie found out about their plans? Did she listen at doors? Sal wouldn't put it past her.

'Ain't I given you a roof over your head and looked after you like you was my own daughter?' Queenie pleaded in a simper.

Sal said nothing in reply to that falsehood.

Queenie's eyes hardened. 'Be down in five minutes or I'll want to know the reason why. And be prepared to work your butt off this evening.'

As Queenie went out, Sal called her several names under her breath. One of these days and soon the old woman would get what was coming to her.

In the meantime – Darren had escaped! Her heart lifted.

It wasn't true that he'd left her in the lurch. He'd had no choice but to run away. Now he'd escaped, he'd soon let her know where she could join him and they could then head for California.

And if he didn't, Sal the Gal would want to know the reason why.

CHAPTER THREE

$100 Reward Money was offered for the capture – dead or alive – of Darren Norton.

Gustavus Greeley had set out after Norton as soon as he could.

$100 was a lot of money; more than Greeley usually earned on a bounty. Everyone must surely want Norton caught and brought to trial. Or brought back to Serenity over the back of a horse to be buried in a pine box. Even more important than the money was the fact that his quarry was just the type of reckless idiot Greeley liked to see punished.

Greeley had been raised to be honest, hard-working and well mannered. He couldn't abide those like Norton who never did a day's work but lived by cheating, robbery and causing trouble and grief for others. Those who got so drunk they lost all control with the result that a young man had been shot dead over a poker hand.

Gustavus was twenty-seven. He was tall and lean. His black hair curling almost to his shoulders, black moustache and blue eyes attracted women of all kinds.

He'd never meant to become a bounty hunter. He, like his father before him, had every intention of being a farmer with his own land. Then one day his father had been in the wrong place at exactly the wrong time: shot dead by a man robbing the local store for a couple of dollars. Gustavus decided to chase down the killer and make him face the consequences of his actions. So far he hadn't caught the man who'd changed his life overnight – he would search till he did – but he had become good at catching others.

He always hoped to bring in his bounty alive so they could stand trial in a court of law but, if they wanted to make a big deal of it, dead was OK too.

It hadn't taken him long to get on Norton's trail. Especially as, like others of his kind, Norton wasn't very bright. Once he'd eluded the posse and believed he was free and clear from pursuit, he'd gotten careless and mostly left a track a mile wide. And who knew why he wasn't making a run for Mexico, which is what any normal person would do. But then most lawbreakers weren't normal; that was why they broke the law in the first place.

'Got you!' he now said in triumph.

'Who the hell are you?' Darren Norton was getting desperate.

He was also exhausted, grubby and hungry. Water in the foothills wasn't a problem, there being plenty of streams and waterholes, but food certainly was. Second day out he'd stolen some grub from a store in a tiny hamlet but, of course, he hadn't thought of rationing it and now there was none left.

He was angry with himself and sorry for himself too. He

should never have shot Arthur. It had been a crazy, stupid thing to do. Not for the first time he'd cursed himself for a fool. Now he was paying the price.

Once he fled Serenity and escaped Rayner and the posse in the foothills he believed he was safe.

No such luck! Marshal Rayner had obviously alerted the law about him.

His original idea had been to escape to Mexico. He should have kept to that. Instead, after believing he'd evaded capture, the thought of crossing the desert, with the weather and the land so hot and dry, and then ending up in a foreign country where he couldn't speak the language and didn't know any of its customs, hadn't seemed such a good plan after all. It was too much of an effort. He'd decided, as he usually did, to take the easy way out.

Then, thinking to catch a train at a lonely way station, he'd been seen and chased and only just managed to flee in time. So he gave up on that idea too.

In fact he hadn't known what to do, with the result that he was still in the foothills.

Then things got even worse.

Someone was on his trail. A lawman perhaps or a bounty hunter. Was there a reward out on him? Whoever it was, he was cleverer and smarter than Rayner, good at tracking and not about to give up. He didn't seem to need either food or rest. Ever since spotting him, Norton had been constantly on the run, trying to outwit his pursuer, without success.

The man was always right there behind him, just out of rifle range, hounding him into doing what he didn't want to do, forcing him to go places he didn't want to go. It began to seem the man knew the moves he was going to make before he even started to make them.

The fact that he hadn't actually caught up with him yet made Norton wonder if the bastard was toying with him.

Once he thought he'd given his pursuer the slip only to wake up in the morning to see a familiar spiral of dust from a horse and rider coming ever closer.

His luck changed when he crossed a fast-flowing river early yesterday. Since then he'd seen no sign of his pursuer, no dust from his horse or smoke from a campfire. Hopefully the bastard had drowned in it. Where he came out of the water, he'd spent some time carefully wiping away his tracks. Even a good tracker couldn't follow a trail that wasn't there.

And shortly afterwards, he'd come across a cave. It made a good hiding place, somewhere to hole up and rest. Now he stood in the shade caused by the cave's overhang, peering hard along his back trail. No one and nothing moved.

'Thank God for that,' he whispered.

He was safe, he could sleep soundly. With a sigh he sank down to the ground, resting his head on his knees. He could take the time to decide what to do next.

Not that he could take too long – the hunter might find him again, there might be others on his trail – but as luck would have it, he'd somehow arrived back quite close to Serenity. The town was just over the next range of hills. Three, four days away at most. Sal the Gal was there. Even he wouldn't be stupid enough to actually go back to the town itself, he'd be recognized for certain, but surely he could get a message to Sal at Queenie's brothel. And Sal, being Sal, would then find a way to come to him.

She would know how to get him out of this mess. She'd also know how they could best reach California where she had planned their new life together. And while Norton wasn't altogether sure that he wanted that life – he liked bumming around with no responsibilities – at least in California he would be safe from pursuit. Once there he could decide what to do next.

As he lay down to sleep, Norton felt quite happy. Things were going to work out OK after all.

Once he realized he was being followed, Norton had done everything he could outwit his pursuer. He had no chance. Although after making his trail difficult to follow yesterday, he probably thought he'd succeeded. Greeley was too smart to be fooled and now he watched from his vantage point near to Norton's hide-out. He'd been waiting for some hours until dawn, which in his experience was the best time to surprise an outlaw. It was when they least expected to be confronted. When they were asleep and at their most vulnerable.

Dawn was little more than a slight brightening in the eastern sky, way over beyond the hills when Greeley started to make his way down to the cave that nestled near the bottom of the slope. He went carefully, not wanting to slip on a rock or trip over the roots of a bush. He didn't want to risk an injury or make any noise to alert his prey.

He'd watched Norton secure his horse to a tree amongst some dense undergrowth just below the cave, out of sight. He gave the animal a wide berth so as not to disturb it.

Pausing just outside the entrance to the cave, he drew his gun. This was the dangerous bit. If Norton was awake or had sensed his approach then for a moment Greeley would be outlined against the sky and make an easy target. Taking a deep breath, he stepped quickly and silently inside, immediately ducking to one side. Nothing! He stopped again, allowing his eyes to get used to the darkness.

The wanted man had made camp right at the back of the cave where his fire couldn't be seen from outside. The slight glimmer of the fire's remains was enough to help Greeley make out, just beyond the ashes, Norton's sleeping shape. He was on his back, mouth open, snoring lightly. A holster and six-shooter lay nearby.

Greeley inched closer. He leant across Norton, who didn't stir, and picked up the holster and gun, putting them down out of reach and harm's way.

Then he kicked at Norton's legs very hard and in a loud voice said, 'Wake up!' He stepped out of the way so that Norton couldn't make a grab for him.

The young man came awake with a startled snort and a yelp of pain. 'What the hell!' He sat up, looking befuddled for a moment, and then, as he realized someone was standing on the other side of the fire – and who it must be – reached out for his gun.

'It ain't there.'

'Shit!' Norton started to scrabble to his feet.

'Shouldn't bother iffen I was you.' Greeley cocked his gun, the sound loud as it echoed around the cave walls. 'I can shoot you dead, and I will, before you can get to me.' Norton collapsed back down. 'That's better. Tell me, are you going to behave yourself?'

He nodded in defeat. Greeley signalled to him and he put both hands out in front of him, allowing himself to be handcuffed. Once done, Greeley grabbed hold of Norton's jacket collar, hauling him up.

'Name's Greeley,' he said. 'I'm a bounty hunter, not a lawman. So, yeah, that means I'm only interested in the reward money. You're worth an awful lot to me and I intend to collect on you. Those who put it up want you dead or alive. I'm not particularly worried either way. It's up to you. You can come with me peaceably enough or I can shoot you and take you back slung face-down over your horse's saddle. But whichever it is, I'm hauling your sorry ass back to Serenity.'

Norton's shoulders slumped in defeat and despair. He'd been so sure he'd lost his pursuer. It wasn't fair.

All the same, they hadn't yet reached Serenity. Norton knew that once there and in jail he'd soon stand trial for murder and hang. The very thought gave him shivers. But it was a long journey back to the town and if he could fool this damn lawman into thinking he'd given up then, maybe, just maybe, he could find a way to escape.

'Good, thought that'd be your answer.' Greeley had a feeling from the look in the other's eyes that while he had no doubt of his ability to handle Norton without too much trouble, he'd have to watch his back because his prisoner might, if he was lucky or desperate enough, get the better of him. After all what did Norton have to lose? He was going back to face the hangman. He might prefer to take his chances out in the open and either try to kill his captor and escape or die by a bullet.

'A word of warning. Don't try to escape. I'm a good shot and, after what you did, I'd sure like an excuse to shoot you. And what I most certainly am not is a fool. So don't take me for one.'

Norton swore to himself. The bounty hunter was as hard and ruthless as he looked. And experienced. He wouldn't stand any nonsense.

DAMN!

CHAPTER FOUR

'Any news?' Frank Evans looked up as Rayner came into the office.

The marshal took off his Stetson and sat down at his desk, shaking his head as he did so. 'No, nothing in yet. Don't look so worried. Mr Greeley's only been after Norton for a few days and from all I've heard about him once he gets on someone's trail he doesn't give up the chase easily. We'll have a hanging to look forward to before too long.'

Evans grinned. 'It can't come soon enough.'

The two lawmen weren't the only ones waiting anxiously for news. So was Sal the Gal.

The day after Darren Norton fled Serenity, she started to make plans.

She couldn't wait to leave Queenie's where life was becoming intolerable with the madam taunting her every day about her 'lost love' and how worthless he'd proved to be.

'I always knew he'd do you wrong,' she said, cackling her horrible cackle. 'And now that a reward has been offered and I've heard there's already a bounty hunter on his trail, it won't be long before he's dragged back here. He'll hang then. Won't that be a sight for sore eyes! Serve the sonofabitch right.'

And because Sal rarely reacted to what Queenie said except to stand, hands on hips, staring at her, the madam was punishing her for her insolence by making her work harder than any of her other girls.

Sal, who was under no illusions about Darren's stupidity, had thought that once a bounty hunter, interested only in collecting the reward, got after him, it was only too likely that he would soon be captured and brought back to Serenity. After all the things she'd decided they would do together, she also decided that she must find a way to rescue him.

If that proved impossible then he'd just have to face up to the consequences of his foolish actions. She would do as she normally did and think only of herself. Forget all about Darren. Leave Serenity far behind. Shame, but there it was, a girl had to look out for herself.

She'd quickly realized that the best time and chance to effect a rescue would be before Darren and the bounty hunter reached Serenity because once he was in the marshal's cells it would be difficult, if not impossible, to break him out. Rayner and Evans respected the law – no way could she bribe them with money or her body to let him go. There would doubtless be several townsmen willing to help the marshal stand guard. With anger still in the air, others might try to lynch Darren and Rayner might not bother to prevent them. And, despite his good looks and happy-go-lucky charm, even Darren wasn't worth the risk of her being arrested, getting shot or otherwise hurt by outraged citizens.

Out in the open she could use her guile and wits to fool his captor.

And while Rayner and Evans were immune to any promises she might make them, others weren't. So one morning when it was quiet she slipped out of the brothel and made her way to the telegraph office. Greg Morgan, the operator, was not the sort to leave his post. He was sure to be there.

Morgan was a tubby man in his forties. He was married to a prune-faced woman who controlled both him and his purse-strings, so that while he was desperate for some real loving, which he didn't get at home, he couldn't afford to visit any sort of brothel and certainly not Queenie's where prices were high. Sal knew that the promise of a visit to her bed, for free, would mean he'd do whatever she asked.

She found him alone. Shutting and locking the door behind her, she kissed him several times then asked if he'd heard anything about Darren Norton and the bounty hunter on his trail.

'No,' Morgan said breathlessly. 'Nothing's come in.'

Good!

'You will let me know when you do hear, won't you? Please. If you're willing to help me, I'll be very willing to do whatever you want.' Sal flashed her eyes saucily at him. 'And I promise Queenie won't make you pay.'

'Well, er, I don't know about that,' Morgan stuttered, blushing a bright red. 'It's against the rules. I do something like that I could lose my job. Perhaps I could do something else for you.'

What else exactly! Sal hid a sigh of exasperation. What else did Morgan have to offer someone like her?

'But no one will ever know. I won't tell anyone. I'd never get you into trouble. So what harm can it do? I'd be awfully appreciative.' Sal stepped closer and kissed the man again.

'You'll let me, you know?' Morgan's voice and hands were trembling. 'For free. Really?'

What did the idiot think she was offering? Coffee and cake? 'Of course I will. It'll be your reward.'

'All right then, Sal, just for you. We can't, well you know, now I suppose?'

'No, sweetheart.' Sal made her voice regretful. 'I've got to get back before Queenie misses me.' That at least was true. Queenie rarely let any of her girls out on their own in case they ran away or entertained a man without her knowledge and so kept all the money.

Morgan sighed in disappointment and looked sulky.

'Don't fret, sweetheart. I'll give you a real good time. One you won't ever forget.'

'All right. I'll do what you want.'

Idiot, Sal thought again, as she sashayed out of the office. Men were so easy to fool and beguile.

Morgan wasn't the only one. Old Man Henderson at the livery said she could take a horse from the stables whenever she wanted and he wouldn't stop her or report her – why he'd even saddle it up for her! She also had to kiss him several times in return. Mr Henderson was ancient and a bit smelly but no worse than some of Queenie's other clients so it was a price worth paying.

She returned to the brothel a little lighter at heart.

She'd already packed a bag with the clothes she would need in her new life, with or without Darren: some underwear, shoes and a couple of her best dresses. In it as well went her knife and the gun she kept in her room for protection against possibly violent customers. The bag was well hidden at the back of the closet. She had also decided what she would wear when she made her escape from the brothel: the few ordinary clothes she owned that wouldn't call attention to her or betray her profession. She kept them with the bag as well.

For a long while now, ever since she'd come up with the idea of going into business for herself, she'd been stealing as much money as she could from her clients without them noticing or caring, and from what she had to hand over to Queenie, definitely without her noticing, because she would most certainly care.

Now all she could do was wait. Sal wasn't very good at waiting and she hoped she would hear something soon. Either that Darren was caught and she could put her plans into action or that, by some miracle, he'd gotten away.

She would give it a few more days, a week at most, and then she would go to San Francisco by herself. It was a long way to go alone but Sal wasn't afraid; she wasn't afraid of anything – not any more, not since the day her father lay dead at her feet, unable to hurt her ever again. Once there she was sure to find some man who took her fancy and who would help her get what she wanted and deserved out of life.

And before she left she would get her own back on Madam Queenie.

31

CHAPTER FIVE

'Mister, it ain't half sweltering,' Norton whined. 'Can't we rest up?'

It was late morning on the day after Greeley had taken Norton prisoner when they finally came down out of the hills and reached the valley. It had been hot enough in the foothills but now it was stifling. The air was sultry, a strong hot wind ruffling the grass and, although the sun was shining, the sky had a molten, heavy look.

Both men were sweating and uncomfortable, although Greeley made several stops so they could take a drink of the warm, brackish water in the canteens and to let the horses rest. He'd kept the animals to a walk, for fear of losing them otherwise.

If the weather didn't improve it was going to take much longer to reach Serenity than Greeley had hoped or expected. And he didn't think he could put up with much more of Norton's endless complaining.

A short while later a jumble of buildings appeared on the horizon. They were approaching a small fort. It consisted of little more than a parade-ground, with barracks for the cavalrymen, officers' quarters, an office or two, some work buildings and stables. There was no stockade or look-out tower.

The fort's original purpose must have been to guard the valley against attack by Apaches. But as far as Greeley was aware there had never been much Indian trouble around here and these days the fort probably had little or no purpose. The garrison was likely to be without a full complement of men. Someone in charge would get around to remembering it one day and decide that it could be put of commission; until then here it stayed.

But doubtless it would be linked to the telegraph. He could send a message to Marshal Rayner telling him he was on his way with Norton.

The sign above the post headquarters announced it as Fort Benton.

Apart from the ringing sound of a blacksmith hard at work in his forge, it was very quiet. But as they came to a stop outside the headquarters building, a young corporal hurried up to take care of their horses, saluting smartly. Obviously, despite the lack of threat, a watch out was still being kept, just in case.

Greeley stepped up onto the veranda that ran all the way round the building, providing shade and somewhere to sit of an evening. He caught hold of Norton's arm, pulling him after him. When he knocked on the door and went inside, he was greeted by a sergeant, who looked old and grizzled enough to be a veteran of the Indian Wars: an old-time cavalryman who stood up on their entrance, ready for trouble.

'I'd like to see your Commanding Officer. I've got

something to ask him,' Greeley said. 'Can you keep an eye on my prisoner for me?'

The sergeant grinned. 'I'd be delighted. He won't get away from me.'

Greeley was quite sure Norton wouldn't even think of trying to do so and would be a fool if he did.

Greeley was then shown into the office of Captain Chambers, who was a youngish man of about thirty-five. He had an air of dissatisfaction about him, which was understandable if he'd joined the army for excitement and to fight Indians, and instead ended up here at Fort Benton, where neither was likely. He might also have hoped for promotion and preferment but they weren't likely either.

'Yes, Mr Greeley, we heard all about the shooting,' he said once Gustavus had introduced himself and told him who his prisoner was. 'We were asked to keep a look out for Norton if he should come this way. Pity he didn't. I could have sent my Apache scouts after him to chase him down. They'd have soon got on his trail and it would have given them something stimulating to do, instead of sitting round here all day.' He sighed. 'So how can I help you?'

'If you have a telegraph here I'd like to send a telegram to Marshal Rayner at Serenity.'

'Of course. I'll get my sergeant to take you across. But, first, I'm just about to have my midday meal, why don't you join me? It'll be nothing fancy, just beef, potatoes and squash.'

'Sounds good to me.' He'd been living off slender rations for days now.

'In exchange you can tell me all about how you captured

Norton. It's not often we hear the news at first hand all the way out here.' Chambers stuck his head out of the door. 'Sergeant. Take the prisoner over to the guardhouse and get him something to eat.' He turned back to Greeley. 'Be little more than slop I'm afraid.'

Both men grinned.

Over a delicious meal, Greeley told the captain all about the chase through the hills. He made it sound more thrilling than it had, in fact, been. 'Now I've just got to get the bastard back to Serenity and hand him over to the law.' He glanced out of the window. 'Bit worried about this weather. It's so damn hot and the air's breathless and the horses are finding it hard to cope. It's unnatural, especially for this time of the year.'

'I think you might soon have more than the heat to worry about.' Chambers poured out mugs of coffee and offered Greeley a cheroot. 'My scouts tell me that there's a real bad storm on the way and it's going to hit very hard and last some while. I've never known them to be wrong. If it's as bad as they warn, there'll be a real danger of flash flooding and landslips and such. Especially in the hills on the approach into Serenity.'

Greeley frowned; he didn't like the sound of that. 'I don't know the area well either. Got any suggestions? I want to be rid of Norton as quick as I can.'

Chambers thought for a moment. 'Well you could take the long way round the edge of the foothills. You'd be on the flat most of the way, but it would add several days to your journey.'

Greeley frowned; that didn't sound like a good idea either.

35

'So my advice would be to ride for Talbot. That's not anywhere near as far as Serenity and it's a much easier ride too, just across the valley as it's situated this side of the hills. And from there you can catch the stagecoach. Wells Fargo will do everything in their power to run the stage. It'll probably add a couple of days to your journey but when the storm does hit you'd be slowed up anyway and I should say that in the end it'll likely be quicker and easier on the stage. It'll be safer too than being out in the open on horseback on your own with just you and your prisoner and the added risk of suffering an accident.'

Greeley considered what the man had said. He didn't much like taking the stage, much preferring to ride and be independent of timetables and scheduled routes. But in this case the captain was likely right. An accident during a storm could mean losing horses or prisoner. Or he might be the one to suffer the accident and find himself at Norton's mercy. At least on the stage he could, if necessary, ask for the help of the driver and the guard in handling his prisoner.

'When's the next stage due?'

'I'm not exactly sure. My sergeant will know. He knows everything.'

The sergeant did know. 'There's a stage leaves Talbot on Thursday morning. You catch that, you'll reach Serenity late Friday.'

It was now Wednesday afternoon.

'We'll leave right after I've send my message,' Greeley decided.

CHAPTER SIX

The telegraph operator's boy flung open the door to Marshal Rayner's office and shouted, 'Telegram for you, marshal!'

Rayner looked up from his desk where he was writing up tax notices. The boy was so excited he was hardly able to keep still but bounced from one foot to the other, all the while waving the piece of paper he held in the air.

'Give it to me,' Rayner ordered. 'D'you know what it says?'

'Yes sirree, marshal.' The boy's face lit up with an enormous grin. 'Darren Norton has been caught! He's on his way back here as a prisoner of one Mr Gustavus Greeley!'

Evans immediately got up from his chair and came round to Rayner's desk, peering over his shoulder. 'Is it true?'

'Sure is!'

'Don't let anyone else know about this,' Rayner warned the boy. 'Tell Mr Morgan the same. It's confidential. You know what means, don't you?'

'Sure do and no, sir, I won't say a word.'

The messenger dashed out again still so thrilled at the news that Rayner, watching him go, doubted he'd be able to keep his promise. Perhaps it didn't matter. The news was certain to be all over Serenity before long anyway. It would be impossible to keep something like this quiet. What he didn't want was some of the hot-heads in town getting together and deciding to lynch Norton before he could be locked up in a cell. Rayner had never lost a prisoner yet and while he wanted the young man to hang, he wanted it done legally.

'What does it say? Where's it from?' Evans was almost as excited as the messenger. 'How soon will they get here?'

'It's come from Fort Benton.'

'Where's that?'

'T'other side of the hills just beyond Talbot.' Rayner read the message out loud. 'It says: "Norton caught. Stop. Will catch stage from Talbot. Stop. Greeley. Stop." '

Evans frowned. 'I wonder why they're travelling by stage.'

'Perhaps Greeley is worried about the weather.' Rayner glanced out of the window. Everyone was beginning to get worried. 'And being out alone with his prisoner in it.'

'Won't going to Talbot take much longer than coming straight here?'

'Yeah, but not by much. He must have decided the stage is his safest bet. Don't blame him. It could get rough out there.'

'I didn't think the little bastard would ever be caught.' Evans sighed in relief.

'I was beginning to wonder myself. And he would probably have gotten away if he'd made a break for Mexico.

Greeley couldn't have followed him there. Instead he must've been riding round in circles to end up being caught so near to Serenity.'

'Norton probably don't know his east from his west!' Evans said with a grin.

Rayner tapped the telegram. 'I'd better send a message about this to Judge Quinn. Even if he's busy conducting other trials on the circuit, I expect he'll do his utmost to get here as fast as he can. He's always saying how concerned he is about the lack of law and order in the Territory and he'll want to hold Norton's trial quickly so as to show everyone we don't tolerate the shooting of men in cold blood.'

The marshal wanted it held soon as well; put an end to the whole sorry business. And he wanted no one but Quinn to sit in judgment so that there could be no doubt about the sentence. Quinn was not known as the Hanging Judge for nothing.

'When's the next stage due in from Talbot, Frank?'

Evans went back to his desk and rummaged about in the top drawer until he came up with a Wells Fargo timetable. 'Umm,' he studied it for a moment. 'Next one is due late Friday afternoon. Leaves Talbot early Thursday.'

'OK.' Rayner thought for a moment. 'It's a fairly straightforward journey from Fort Benton to Talbot and so long as Greeley doesn't encounter any problems on the way he should get there in time to catch it. Just to make sure we're ready for them, I'll send a message to the Wells Fargo office and ask them to let us know if Greeley and his prisoner are on that particular stage and if it's running to schedule.'

Forewarned and forearmed was one of Rayner's mottoes.

'Wells Fargo won't delay the stage for anyone or anything. It'll run even if Greeley's not on it.'

'I know. That's not why I'm taking precautions.'

'What is it then, Marshal?'

'I just want us to be ready to stop anyone trying to take the law into their own hands. I want this done right in a court of law. So on your rounds can you listen out for any wild talk?' Rayner knew he could rely on Frank. He might hate Norton for what he'd done, but he was too good a lawman not to want the young man to be convicted by judge and jury.

'Sure thing. Are you going to tell Mr Hamlin?'

Rayner nodded. 'I'd better. Before he hears the news from someone else. I'll go once I send off the telegrams.'

'Is it all right if I ride out and tell Irene? She and her family will want to know as well.'

'Yeah, OK. Don't dally there though. I need you here in town.'

These days Rayner always approached Hamlin's Gun & Ammunition Store with a guilty feeling of foreboding. Although others, including Hamlin himself, had said he wasn't responsible for what Norton had done, he still felt partly at fault for Arthur's killing. And always would.

He'd been an experienced lawman long enough to know that Darren Norton was a ne'er-do-well. He should have found an excuse to run him out of town; that way there would have been no shooting and Arthur would still be alive. Instead he'd done nothing and simply hoped that Norton would tire of Serenity and leave of his own accord.

He hadn't. Now it was too late and a decent young man was dead, leaving a father and a fiancée to mourn him.

As he walked from the telegraph office to the store, it was quiet and the streets were almost empty, except for the usual old men loafers sitting in the shade of the veranda in front of the hotel and some businessmen gathered outside the bank. Clearly no one else had as yet heard the news.

Artie Hamlin was alone in his store. He was wiping down the counter where several shiny new pistols were displayed. On the wall behind him in a locked cabinet he kept the rifles. Ammunition was in another cabinet. It was a well-stocked store and well ordered but Hamlin's heart was no longer in running it, now he didn't have a son to leave it to.

Since Arthur's murder he'd suddenly looked much older than his forty-five years. His hair had turned grey almost overnight and his eyes were sunken and face lined as if he rarely slept. He'd also lost weight and his suit hung on him.

He'd never get over his son's unnecessary and pointless death but surely seeing the killer swinging at the end of a rope would help.

'Howdy, Charley, what can I do for you?' Hamlin put down his duster. He tried to smile. 'What is it?'

'Good news, Artie. A bounty hunter has made a prisoner of Darren Norton and is at this minute bringing him back to Serenity.'

'Oh.' Hamlin slumped forward.

'Here.' Rayner hurried round the counter to catch hold of the man before he fell. He led him to the customer's chair in the corner. 'Sit down. Breathe deep. Can

41

I get you anything?'

He went to turn the sign on the door to closed, so that Hamlin could recover in private without any customers coming in and disturbing him with excited gossip. And a lot of people would surely be heading this way once they heard.

After a moment Hamlin gasped, 'No, no, I'm fine. It was a shock is all.'

Despite Hamlin's protests that he was all right, his face was grey and he was having trouble breathing, so Rayner went through to the back and found where the man stored his bottle of whiskey. He poured out a shot and handed Hamlin the glass. 'Drink this. It'll do you good.'

Hamlin did as he was told and a little colour returned to his cheeks. 'When will they get here?'

'They're coming by stage from Talbot and hopefully they'll catch the one that gets in on Friday. I've sent a message to Judge Quinn. Don't worry, Artie, once this is over, you'll be able to rest easier at night.' And so would Rayner.

'Charley.' Hamlin reached out a shaky hand to catch hold of the marshal's jacket. 'Do you think that either you or young Frank could ride out and meet the stage? I don't want anything to go wrong, not now. I don't want the slippery bastard getting away somehow. I want to see him punished for what he did. Will you do that for me?'

'I don't see why not.'

'And will you ask Frank to ride out to the farm and tell Arthur's girl and her folks the news?'

'He's on his way right now.'

'Good. Poor Irene has taken this real hard. Frank is

proving to be a good friend to her just as he was to Arthur.'

Rayner nodded. He wondered whether, after a suitable period of mourning, Frank might court Irene. He hoped so. They were both nice young people and deserved some happiness.

In the meantime, all he had to do was hope that the weather held, that Wells Fargo was able to run the stage and that nothing happened between now and Friday or between Talbot and here.

Surely, that wasn't too much to ask!

CHAPTER SEVEN

'Hey, Sal. Sal, you there?'

A pebble or two struck Sal the Gal's bedroom window and woke her up. Yawning she got out of bed and reached for her wrap. She went over to the window and pushed up the sash, peering out. Greg Morgan. The telegraph operator stood below looking up expectantly. Was he here with news or just the hope she would take pity on him and invite him up to her room? Whatever it was, it had just better be worth disturbing her rest over, especially as the afternoon was so hot she'd found it difficult to get to sleep in the first place.

She leant out of the window far enough to let him see she had nothing on underneath the wrap.

'What is it, Greg?' She made herself sound enthusiastic and loving.

'Just heard, Sal.' News! 'Norton's been captured and he's due to be brought back here on the stage from Talbot.'

'Really? The stage?' That was a surprise.

'It must have something to do with the storm that everyone says is due to strike any day now.'

Of course. 'When will they get here? Do you know?'

'Yeah, I checked the stage timetable for you, Sal.'

God, did the man want a medal? 'Well?'

'The next stage is due on Friday. It leaves Talbot early on Thursday morning.'

'Does the marshal know?' Morgan nodded. 'You told him? Before me?' Sal's tone hardened.

A whine came into the man's voice as he began to babble. 'I wasn't alone when the message came in. I couldn't stop my lad from seeing it. Otherwise I'd've kept the news quiet and told you first. Honestly I would. He ran off with it to old Rayner before I could stop him. I'm real sorry, Sal. Does it matter?'

'No, Greg, it's not important, don't worry.'

Rayner learning the news before her wasn't a problem. He didn't know she had plans.

'I wouldn't want to get you into trouble with the law, not when you've been so very helpful. You've done your best.'

The man's face lit up. 'Does that mean you'll, you know, this evening?'

'It's what I promised, ain't it? I'll make the risks you're taking for me worthwhile, you see if I don't. Yeah, Greg darling, you come back here tonight and ask for me. And tell Queenie you ain't got to pay. She'll send you up to my room. Where I'll be waiting. I'll make sure you ain't disappointed.'

'Couldn't I come now?'

'No, sweetheart, I'm busy. Your wait will make it even

more worthwhile.' Sal blew the man a kiss and allowed him a glimpse of her naked breasts.

He went off with a smile and a spring in his step which made her laugh. Poor sap! As if Queenie would let in any customer without the means to pay in his pocket. As if Sal would let just anyone have her body for nothing. As far as both women were concerned, there was no such thing as a free ride!

Sal sat on the bed, thinking hard.

Friday . . . that should give her enough time. But she'd have to move fast.

After hastily dressing in the old clothes she'd put by, she dragged the carpetbag out from the back of the closet. The purse containing some of her money she hid in the deep inside pocket of her jacket where it would be safe. The rest was stored in the bottom of the bag. She tucked her gun into the belt of her skirt and put the knife in her jacket pocket, where she could get at both easily.

Despite the urgency of the situation she wasn't leaving the brothel just yet. While she had enough money to start her new life in California, she could always do with more and, after all, she'd certainly earned it.

Besides, Queenie deserved to be punished. And because the madam loved money above everything else, stealing everything she had would be the best punishment to inflict on her.

Carefully Sal opened the bedroom door. The brothel was always quiet in the afternoon. The other girls and Queenie would be asleep. She tiptoed along the passage and peered over the stair-rail. No sign of the bouncer. He could be anywhere. Sal had no idea what he did during the day. She fingered her gun. She'd be more than willing to use it if necessary.

Avoiding the stair that creaked, she made her way down the stairs and along the hall to Queenie's office at the back of the house. It was where the madam kept her papers and her money. From the very beginning Sal had made sure she learnt Queenie's secrets and she knew the cash was kept in a tin box in the locked bottom drawer of the desk, while the key to the box stayed in the top drawer.

It wasn't exactly a thief-proof system, but then Queenie probably never dreamt anyone would dare rob her, especially one of 'her girls'. Queenie was so certain she had them cowed sufficiently that they would never dare cross her. That might be true of the rest. It wasn't true of Sal. The madam was in for a nasty surprise.

Sal closed the office door with a quiet click and went over to the desk. Both drawers were locked but it was a matter of moments to use her knife to open them. The blade left several scratches behind but so what? She hoped Queenie would be upset at the damage.

There was the small key, hidden under some correspondence, and there was the large tin box. As she pulled it out, it felt quite heavy. Hopefully it contained several days' takings. Queenie wasn't exactly a welcome customer at the bank and only went there to deposit money once or twice a week.

Sal unlocked the box. What she saw made her eyes gleam. Coins and notes spilled out. Swiftly she stuffed the carpetbag with as much as she could. Time later, when she was safely away, to count it, sort it out and hide it properly with the rest of the money.

'What the hell do you think you're doing?'

Sal swung round. Queenie, a furious look on her face, hands on her hips, stood in the doorway.

'What does it look like?' Sal grinned. She threw some coins at Queenie, catching her in the face with them.

'You little thief!' Queenie then made a mistake. Instead of calling for help, she came further into the room, obviously believing she could handle Sal herself.

Sal grinned again, making the madam even angrier. 'I'm taking what's mine and what's yours too.'

'Oh no you ain't! I'll deal with you good and proper. Make you sorry you were ever born.' Queenie reached for the heavy cane she kept by the desk. 'I've been longing to do this for ages. It's what you deserve, Miss High and Mighty.' She advanced on Sal, raising the cane, a furious look on her face.

Before she could strike her, Sal acted first. She threw a roundhouse punch that caught Queenie square on the jaw, her ring cutting into the woman's skin. Queenie's head flew back and her eyes glazed over instantly. She collapsed onto the carpet and lay still. Sal kicked her once or twice. Then bending down she tore strips from the woman's petticoat, fashioning a gag and strips to tie her hands and feet. She wasn't gentle about any of it.

She considered knifing her. But letting her live with the knowledge of what had been done to her was even better. Queenie would be left without any money and, with everyone knowing she was vulnerable, she'd be a laughing stock. Hopefully the other girls would seize their chance to flee her house and go somewhere better, leaving her with nothing.

After taking every single last coin, Sal crept to the door. Still no sounds, although she thought she heard someone stirring upstairs. Queenie opened her eyes and made a gurgling sound as she tried to get up.

'Don't!' Sal kicked her again.

Queenie, a scared look on her face, collapsed back down on the floor, aware that her one-time employee meant business.

Clutching her bag Sal walked along the hall to the front door. With freedom so close, her heart began to thump and her mouth turned dry. One hand touched her gun. She wasn't about to be stopped now.

Bolts secured the door, top and bottom. They slid back easily and noiselessly. With a little sigh of relief, she stepped outside – free and clear. There was no pursuit.

Without looking back, she ran down the street towards the stables. She'd done it! Mr Henderson would saddle a horse for her in exchange for more kisses and she'd be away. She could escape Serenity and go and find Darren. Rescue him and start out for California.

It was what she deserved.

CHAPTER EIGHT

It was still dark when Greeley forced his prisoner to wake up and start on the last part of the journey to Talbot. Before they'd got far, the wind began to howl wildly and heavy black clouds scudded across the sky. It turned bitterly cold. Captain Chambers was right when he warned of a terrible storm coming and it looked like the storm would hit during the ride to Serenity. It made Greeley glad he'd decided to take the stage.

That was if they made it to Talbot in time to catch it. Quickly the going became hard and the horses got so jittery that he began to doubt they would.

In the event they reached the town with just thirty or so minutes to spare. The livery stable was just across the way from the Wells Fargo office and there, in the road outside, was the stagecoach. Lights shone from the office window.

Greeley got his rifle and saddlebags from his horse and gave Norton a slight push. 'Let's go.' He'd be glad to get inside.

As he always did when entering a place, his eyes

scanned the room. He saw they weren't the only passengers. A man and woman, husband and wife probably and farmers if their clothes were anything to go by, sat at a table in the far corner, some packages at the man's feet. They glanced up, eyes widening as they saw that Norton was in handcuffs. The farmer's wife looked nervous. Who could blame her? She was about to make a long journey in precarious conditions and now, even worse, had an outlaw for company.

Shoving Norton down at the table as far from the couple as possible, Greeley went up to the counter. 'Is the stage running on time?'

The clerk was a fussy little man with enormous whiskers. 'Yes, sir, of course it is. Wells Fargo doesn't let anything get in the way of its schedule.' Importantly he consulted the clock on the wall behind him. 'Be leaving in twenty minutes time. Would you and your prisoner like some coffee and biscuits while you wait?'

'Please.' Greeley sat down. When the clerk brought over their coffee he said, 'You'd better warn your driver and guard they'll have a wanted man on board.'

'I'll do that,' the clerk said and hurried out the back.

A short while later the door opened again, letting in a blast of cold air, and a young woman in her early twenties stepped inside. She looked bedraggled and some of her fair hair had come loose from its pins and hung untidily around her face. Despite that, Greeley could see she was very pretty with a nice figure. She wore plain travelling clothes and was clutching a large bag.

'Oh, thank goodness I haven't missed the stage,' she said in a small voice. 'The wind was so bad it slowed me down and I feared I'd get here too late.' She glanced around. 'Is this all the passengers? I mean there is still a seat available for me isn't there? Is it running on time?'

'Yes, don't you fret none, miss.' The clerk obviously didn't mind a pretty girl questioning Wells Fargo's timetables. He led her over to the fire. 'Warm yourself up while I get you some coffee. There's seats aplenty and the stage is almost ready to go.'

With a smile the girl paid for her ticket and then putting down her bag, held her hands out to the stove, rubbing them together. She shivered.

'Here, miss, why don't you sit down?' Greeley moved to another chair so she could take that next to the stove.

She lowered her eyes shyly. 'Thank you. Are you a lawman? Is that your prisoner?'

'He's my prisoner, yes, but I'm a bounty hunter, not a lawman.'

'Is he dangerous? Are we in any danger from him?'

'There's no reason for you or anyone else to be scared. He's wearing handcuffs. He can't hurt anyone. He knows I'll deal with him soon enough if he tries.' Greeley wasn't above boasting in front of an attractive young woman. 'Ain't that right?'

Norton nodded, a surly expression on his face.

'What's he done?'

Reluctantly Greeley decided to tell her the truth and hope she wouldn't be too upset. 'He shot and killed a young man in Serenity.' He heard the farmer's intake of breath and saw him glance at his wife.

'How awful!' The girl looked shocked.

The farmer spoke up. 'Is that really the bastard who

shot young Arthur Hamlin?'

'That he is, sir. Darren Norton.'

Norton mumbled something about not having yet been found guilty, but no one took any notice of him.

'Of course we heard all about that, didn't we, Ruthie? But as we don't get into town all that often we didn't know Arthur or his father except on nodding terms.'

'But he always seemed such a nice boy,' his wife added. 'Real polite. His father was devastated at what happened. As was his fiancée, who's the daughter of our nearest neighbours. Irene's such a lovely girl. It was terrible.'

'And we certainly don't know him.' The farmer nodded at Norton. 'Asides from hearing that he often caused trouble in the saloons, drinking and gambling an' such. Places like that should be closed down in my opinion. Look forward to seeing him swinging at the end of a rope.'

Norton said nothing but sat back and closed his eyes, not wanting anyone to see the fear in them; he had a devil-may-care reputation to maintain after all.

He'd been busy during the ride to Talbot plotting ways to escape, each one more elaborate and more unlikely to succeed than the last. It wasn't fair. It wasn't as if he'd meant to shoot Arthur. Especially in front of numerous witnesses, most of whom would be willing to testify against him.

But he had and now that Serenity was getting ever closer he was petrified. There would be no reprieve. He was heading for the scaffold and there he'd be surrounded by jeering, cheering crowds of men and women laughing at his downfall. He could already feel the rope around his neck, tightening, tightening. . . .

Could he escape? There might be a chance. He'd seize it if it came.

After another short wait, the driver, a strong looking man of about fifty, came in. He said his name was Bill Brown and then added, 'Stage is just about ready to leave, folks, if you'd care to get on board. Hang onto your hats, it's gonna be a bumpy ride!' He laughed loudly. 'Even worse, Ray Daniels, my guard, is new to me and he ain't never ridden this route afore. Could be trouble!'

As they went outside the farmer came up to the girl and said, 'Hey, miss, don't I know you from somewhere?'

She looked startled. 'Oh no, sir, I don't think so.'

'Your face is real familiar.'

'No, I . . .'

'For goodness sake, Clarence,' his wife said. She poked him in the side. 'Leave the girl be and let's get on board like the driver said.'

Outside with the wind howling around them, they handed their bags up to the driver who secured them firmly on top. Boarding the coach, Greeley found himself between Norton and the girl, with the farmer and his wife opposite. The driver and his guard settled themselves onto the seat, Brown clicked the horses into a walk and they were off, swaying down Talbot's main street, across some scrubland and out into open countryside.

On the way to Serenity.

CHAPTER NINE

'As we're all travelling to Serenity together, we oughtta introduce ourselves,' the farmer said. 'I'm Clarence Lewis and this here is my wife, Ruth.'

Up close Greeley saw that they were both in their fifties, with sunburnt and leathery skin and work-worn hands. Although it was what he had always wanted and expected to be, he knew a farmer's life wasn't easy, especially out here in Arizona where the weather and the dangers were so extreme.

'Are you on your way home?' he asked.

'That's right. Our farm is just outside Serenity. We've been in Talbot buying some piglets that were up for sale. Thought we'd try something new. Paid a reasonable price too. They'll be following along in the next week or so after they've been weaned. Real pleased with the deal, ain't we, Ruthie?'

The woman didn't have a chance to reply as Lewis hurried on, 'Should make us a real good profit. Pigs don't need much looking after. All they do is eat and sleep. Ruthie also took the chance to meet up with a couple of friends she ain't seen in a while. Women's gossip,' he chuckled. 'Had a good time, didn't you, hon, over coffee and cakes?'

'It was lovely to see them again. We don't see too many people on the farm and anyway we're usually too busy to socialize,' Ruth sighed.

Life on a farm was lonely too, especially for a woman. It was quite likely as well that Lewis's somewhat ornery disposition put visitors off.

She stared out of the coach window and added rather forlornly, 'I wish we'd listened to their warnings about the storm and decided not to go home yet. They said we should stay on in Talbot a couple of days till the worst blew over.'

'Now, Ruthie, think of the cost and you know we're needed back at the farm.'

Lewis sounded like a stubborn individual, who made all the decisions, right or wrong, and never listened to anyone else's advice.

'Can't let our son do all the work. Peter,' he added. 'Good lad. Hard working and law-abiding. Unlike some.' He glanced Norton's way.

'Peter hopes to get married soon,' Ruth said. 'I can't wait for the wedding and then I'm hoping plenty of grandchildren will come along. Children will liven the place up. And it'll be good to have some help around the house.'

'Ruthie is already making baby clothes,' Lewis laughed.

'No, I'm not,' Ruth protested with a blush. 'Don't tease.'

'I think it's nice you'll have female company.' The girl glared at the farmer.

Lewis immediately turned his attention to the girl. 'And you?'

'I'm Miss Fuller. Sarah.'

'Have you come far?' Greeley asked.

Sarah shook her head. 'No, just a few miles down the road.'

'What on earth brings you out in such weather?' Ruth said.

'I'm going to Serenity to be with my sister, Mary. She's expecting her first baby any day now.' She lowered her eyes as if embarrassed about speaking of such a matter before strangers.

'How lovely,' Ruth sighed.

'She wants me to be with her. You see, her husband is a farmer too and he's busy each and every day looking after the land and the animals.' Lewis nodded in agreement to that. 'So Mary asked if I would stay with her for a while to help her once the baby is born.'

'Well I think it's brave of you to travel all that way by yourself.'

'I'd given Mary my word, Mrs Lewis. But I didn't realize the weather was going to be as bad as it was. I thought more'n once that I was going to have an accident and then I was afraid the stage would have left before me.'

Obviously feeling he'd been left out of the conversation long enough, Lewis said, 'Perhaps we know your sister. Mary, you say?'

'Yes, Mary Trent.'

'And she's pregnant?'

'Yes.'

'What's her husband's name?'

'Tom.'

Lewis frowned. 'Nope, don't ring any bells. You sure they live in Serenity?'

'Of course I am. Well, not in Serenity itself because they've got a farm. They're quite a way out of town actually.'

'Still don't know 'em.'

'They haven't long moved there so I dare say they haven't had a chance to introduce themselves to many people yet. That's why I want to be with Mary when she has the baby, so she's not all alone.'

'Even so, the farming community is small and I'd've thought I'd've heard of 'em, which I ain't,' Lewis continued in his stubborn way.

Ruth interrupted. 'We don't know everyone, dear.'

'And you say your folks farm near Talbot?'

Sarah looked uncomfortable at all the farmer's questions and just nodded.

In an effort to stop her husband questioning Sarah so relentlessly, Ruth said, 'Clarence and me came out here in 1871. Clarence fought for the North during the War Between the States and afterwards he couldn't settle to work for his pa. . . .'

'Pa had a carpentry business,' Lewis interrupted. 'The work was OK but we didn't earn a lot and the customers were a demanding lot, who knew nothing about working wood. So after Pa died, I decided to sell up. Start anew. Ruthie and me thought long and hard about what we wanted to do and where we wanted to go.'

'Why become a farmer?' Greeley asked. 'When you had no experience of the life? And why choose Arizona?'

Ruth looked as if she had asked exactly the same questions. Despite what Clarence said, he probably hadn't involved her in any decision-making.

Lewis went on, 'Well, from what we read in the newspapers, it sounded as though farmers were badly needed out this way and there was good land to be had, cheap too, and good money to be made. I'd have my independence. And not only has Arizona plenty of open space, it also has sunshine and warm winters. Not like back in Maine. Winters there were harsh and long.'

'Weren't you scared of the Indian threat or outlaws?'

'No. I didn't think they'd bother us.'

Greeley rolled his eyes at the man's obstinate stupidity. It was just lucky chance they hadn't been attacked, especially in the early days. He knew from bitter experience how perilous life on the frontier could be.

'Never regretted it once, have we, Ruthie?'

'Well, dear, it has been hard going at times and, despite what Clarence says, we certainly haven't become rich on it.'

'There goes my wife again! Always moaning. Don't listen to her. It's a good life and we ain't beholden to no one. What about you?' he turned again to Sarah.

'It's much the same,' she said. 'My father was also in the Union Army and I grew up on a small farm in Ohio. We moved to Talbot when I was fifteen, eight years ago now. Mary is two years older than me and I've got two younger brothers, both of whom want to have farms of their own one day when they're old enough.'

'Do you like living in Arizona?'

'Oh yes, Mrs Lewis, I do. Although you're right,

farming is hard work. It can be dangerous too. So Pa made sure to teach us how to shoot.'

'Well, we ain't never had any trouble.' Not liking to be contradicted, Lewis turned deliberately from Sarah.

He was about to start questioning Greeley, when Ruth said, 'Oh, dear. It's coming over real black. The storm must be approaching. I hoped we'd get to Serenity in time to avoid it but I don't think we will.'

'My wife always looks on the dark side of things.'

Sarah scowled at Lewis for being so unfeeling of his wife's fears and reached across to hold Ruth's hand. 'Don't worry we'll all look out for each other. We'll be safe enough.'

'I surely do hope so.'

CHAPTER TEN

Then what the stagecoach passengers had been expecting and fearing happened. The storm hit with a sudden and ferocious fury.

Lightning forked across the sky in a blinding white light, making them jump, followed instantly by a clap of thunder so loud everything trembled and so prolonged it seemed it would never stop.

Both Sarah and Ruth cried out and Ruth buried her head against her husband's chest, while he put an arm around her.

Buffeted by a blast of strong wind, the stagecoach swayed alarmingly, almost toppling over. The horses set up a terrified whinnying.

'They're going to bolt!' Ruth screamed.

But somehow Brown controlled both them and the coach and sensibly slowed the horses to a walk.

More lightning flashed, sparking the air with electricity, and within moments it started to rain torrentially hard. The dry and arid desert turned instantly into a quagmire and mud spattered up behind the coach's wheels, slowing them even more. It became almost as dark as night.

Sarah caught hold of one of Greeley's hands and held on tight.

'Don't worry,' he said. 'The driver knows what he's doing.'

He hoped he was right. He didn't like admitting it, but he was as frightened as everyone else. It was like nothing he'd ever seen before. He wondered whether they would be able to go on much further as the thunder continued to roar while the rain was so heavy it was almost impossible to see anything beyond the stagecoach's windows.

Marshal Rayner had never known a storm like this one.

When it first struck, he said he'd go out to make sure everyone had locked up tight and to warn people to stay inside. He didn't get very far. He was soaked through as soon as he stepped onto the sidewalk. The wind was so wild he had to cling onto the nearest hitching rail to avoid being knocked off his feet. His ears were assailed with the noise of the incessant thunder. Wisely he decided to go back into the office: the townsmen would have to take their chances. To be out in this was to risk being killed and anyone who didn't realize that was stupid.

Evans poured out coffee for them both and they stood at the window, watching the sheets of rain that made it difficult to see the hitching rail, let alone the other side of the street. A couple of cowboys staggered by, leading their horses to the safety of the livery stable.

'Don't look like it's going to stop any time soon,' the deputy said.

If anything, it was getting worse. The thunder and lightning were almost constant and the rain even harder.

'I reckon we might as well call it a day,' Rayner said. 'Anyone is out in this, well more fool them. We won't be able to do anything until morning. Sal the Gal didn't pick a very good time to rob the madam and run off, did she? Poor old Queenie! Fancy. I know Sal is quite the gal, but I never imagined even she would have the guts to fell Queenie to the ground and steal all her money.'

'Couldn't've happened to a nicer lady! Sal must sure as hell pack a punch.'

The two men grinned at one another. Neither had much time for Queenie; she treated her girls badly and didn't look after them, being concerned only with the money they earned her. They didn't have much time for Sal either, a girl they considered as hard as nails, but they had to admire her for what she had done. Not many people dared cross Queenie.

Summoned to the brothel, they had found the madam, her hair dishevelled, face bruised, jaw already swelling up and one eye almost closed. They'd listened to her screeching complaints and demands that Sal be caught and her and the money returned to the brothel. After calming her down somewhat, the two lawmen had made a half-hearted attempt to find Sal.

They doubted they would. As Rayner said, if she had any sense she'd have high-tailed it out of town as quickly as she could.

They were right. Sal was nowhere around. No one admitted seeing her or knowing what had become of her. However, a little later one of the farmers from nearby came in to report his horse was missing, stolen, from the livery.

Old Man Henderson professed ignorance.

'I don't know as I give much for her chances,' Rayner went on. 'There ain't much shelter out there. I don't suppose even Sal could've reached anywhere she'd be safe before all this started.'

'Guess not.'

Rayner sighed. 'She might've been a whore and a thief, but I can't help feeling sorry for her. It took guts to make good her escape from the brothel and Queenie and now she's ridden straight into a storm.'

'There's those folks on the stagecoach too. They'll certainly have been caught out in the open.'

'Yeah. I hope they're OK.'

After a while the thunder and lightning eased slightly and moved away towards the hills. But it continued to rain hard, the drops bouncing high in the puddles that covered the desert, forming a thick mist. The sky was full of dense, black clouds. The journey became even slower and even more uncomfortable, the stagecoach seeming to hit every hole and bump it came to while being continually rocked by the gusts of wind.

No one said much. They were too apprehensive to make idle talk and they had no desire to talk about the conditions.

But Bill Brown was an experienced driver and able to handle the horses. At least out in the desert. It might be different once they started the climb up through the hills. No one wanted to think about that.

After a couple of hours Lewis broke the silence. He pulled out his watch from his jacket pocket. 'We ain't making very good time. We should've reached the way station long before now. Ain't sure how far we've still got to go.' He cackled. 'Wells Fargo won't be able to boast they've kept to time today, will they?'

'It's not funny, Clarence.'

'Now, Ruthie, don't take on so. You know I don't mean nothing and . . .'

Suddenly from above the driver let out a startled yell and began to haul on the reins in an attempt to bring the horses to a halt.

Ruth screamed as the stagecoach rocked precariously and, as it came to a juddering halt, Sarah was flung from her seat.

'What's happening?' Ruth cried. 'What's wrong?'

Greeley helped Sarah up and stuck his head out of the window.

'What is it?' Lewis demanded.

CHAPTER ELEVEN

Expecting to see some sort of obstruction ahead of them, Greeley was quite surprised. 'There's a man standing by the side of the road,' he announced over his shoulder. 'He's alone.'

At least Greeley couldn't see any sign of anyone else through the rain. The land was flat and empty. No riders waiting in ambush anywhere. Not that that was likely. Surely no one would be so foolish as to try and rob the stage on a day like this, but he was ready to act if they were and his hand rested on the butt of his gun.

'I'll find out who he is.'

He got down from the coach. He landed ankle-deep in the mud and almost fell. At the same time the guard, Daniels, climbed down from his perch, shotgun held under his arm. Not that the young man who'd hailed the coach appeared to pose any threat. He was sopping wet, shivering with the cold and he looked thoroughly dejected and worn out, hardly able to stand up.

'What the hell are you doin' out here?' Daniels demanded. 'On foot and soaked an' all.'

'My horse got spooked by the first flash of lightning and

threw me.' The young man spoke through teeth that chattered so hard it was difficult to understand what he said. 'It then ran off. Left me stranded.'

'Whereabouts was this?'

He pointed shakily to the left. 'Yonder somewhere.'

Greeley said, 'Where were you headed?'

'T . . . T . . . Talbot.'

'Well now it looks like you're on your way to Serenity.' The guard laughed.

'Sir, I don't care where I go so long as I get out of this damn rain. There is room on board, isn't there?' He cast an anxious look at the stage where the faces of Ruth and Sarah stared down at him.

'You can sit on top. . . .'

Greeley interrupted. 'No, he'd be better off inside. Dry off a bit.'

'He'll soak the seats.'

'He can sit on the floor.'

Daniels shrugged as if to say he didn't much care either way.

Greeley climbed back into the stage. 'It's OK. Just someone who got caught out in the storm.' He turned to help the young man up after him. 'Sit down.'

The newcomer did so, wrapping his arms round himself, shivering.

'Oh, you poor boy,' Ruth cried as she saw the bedraggled stranger. 'Here.' She pulled a handkerchief from her pocket. 'Wipe your face with this.'

'Thank you, ma'am.'

'What's your name?' Lewis inevitably asked as the stage set off again. He wanted to know everything.

67

'I'm Harry Anderson, sir.'

Anderson was about twenty-five with dark hair and blue eyes. Normally he would probably be called dapper because he wore a bowler hat, black suit and shoes. Not now. The rim of his hat had collapsed, his trousers stuck to his legs and the shoes looked as if they'd only be fit to throw away. His face and hands were covered with scratches from where he'd fallen off his horse.

Lewis stared at him for a moment or two. 'Ain't I seen you some place else?'

Anderson looked somewhat taken aback at the words, which sounded almost like an accusation. 'I don't think so, sir. I certainly don't recognize you.'

'Take no notice, Mr Anderson. My husband always thinks he's come across everyone he meets.' Ruth frowned at Lewis, who shrugged and grinned.

'What are you doing way out here by yourself?' Greeley asked, still on the alert for trouble.

He didn't altogether trust Anderson and was suspicious of the fact that he just happened to be stranded by the stagecoach road without his horse just as they were coming by so there would be no choice but to take him up. Could he be in league with Norton? Here to help him escape? While it was highly unlikely, word did have a way of getting around and one of Norton's pals might have discovered he was going to be on the Serenity stage and planned to effect a rescue.

Greeley decided to keep a careful eye on both of them, just in case. He wasn't going to lose that $100 bounty if he could help it, nor deprive the citizens of Serenity of their hanging.

'I'm a drummer. In ladies' goods.'

'Where's your stuff?'

'With my horse,' Anderson said ruefully. 'Along with everything else I had with me. I've lost it all. As for my horse, it's still running I expect.'

'How dreadful,' Ruth said.

'I hadn't long picked up and paid for the goods I was meant to sell, for which I used up all the money I'd been saving. I was hoping to make a good profit on 'em too. Now they're all gone. I don't know what I'll do. I've got nothing left.' Anderson groaned and put his head in his hands.

'You're alive, that's what matters,' Sarah said.

Right then Anderson didn't look convinced of the fact. He groaned again. 'For a long while I feared I was lost for sure and about to die out there in the desert. I had no idea which way to go or how far I was from anywhere. I was walking for what seemed like hours. It was only when I came over the ridge and spotted the stagecoach road that I hoped I might be OK.'

'How did you know there was a stagecoach due?' Greeley said.

'I didn't. But I thought if nothing else I could follow the road on foot. It would have to lead somewhere. Eventually. You can't imagine how relieved I felt when I saw you coming. Thank God you stopped.'

'We should be at the way station soon. You can dry off a bit there.'

'I hope so. I've never been so wet or cold in my life.' Anderson slumped back against the door and closed his eyes.

The others were as relieved as Anderson when not much later the way station finally came into view. Up close this proved to be little more than a large adobe hut with a corral to one side for the horses, along with a few work buildings in the yard at the back. It was situated at the base of the foothills, which rose, dark and forbidding in the rain, behind it, the trees swaying in the incessant, still howling wind.

'Isn't it lonely?' Sarah said with a little shudder. 'I wouldn't like to live here.'

As the stagecoach came to a halt, a broad-shouldered young man hurried up to the stage, pulling open the door.

'Howdy, folks, you made it then! All in one piece too.'

'Just about,' Lewis muttered.

'Name's Matt Digby. Go on into the house. My wife has coffee and soup ready that'll warm you up nicely. Hey,' his smile died as he saw Norton's handcuffs. 'He ain't going to be a bother is he?'

'No,' Greeley said. He gave Norton a poke in the back. 'Hurry up.' Then offering Sarah his arm, he said, 'Here, Miss Fuller, let me help you so you don't slip.'

While the passengers trudged through the heavy, clinging mud and disappeared into the shack, Digby went to help the driver and guard with the horses.

'Hi, Bill, wondered if and when you'd get here. You're well and truly late.'

Brown didn't look pleased; he prided himself on always being on time. Now he said, 'Storm started pretty soon after we left Talbot. Made it real tough going.'

'Who's that?' Digby looked at the guard, who was inspecting the luggage.

'Ray Daniels,' Brown grimaced. 'Of all times he's new to me. He usually works further south.'

'What happened to Pete?'

'Not sure exactly. Took sick or something. First time Ray's been this way.'

'And it could be the last,' Daniels added with his own grimace. 'Didn't think anything could be this bad.'

'No,' Brown agreed. 'Even in winter we usually have a pretty clear run. Still the worst is over, I reckon.' He looked up at the sky.

'Down in the desert maybe,' Digby said. 'But I dunno what you'll find the higher you get. Reckon there'll be a flash flood or two and some trees are surely down. You sure you want to go on? Wouldn't it be better to wait until tomorrow at least? Way things are I doubt you'll make it to the next way station before nightfall.'

It was a tight enough schedule normally when the weather was good. Now they could be stuck in the hills in the dark. That wasn't a prospect Brown relished. But he said, 'Lost enough time as it is. Can't afford to lose more.'

'Up to you. Go in and see the wife. Get warmed up. Have something to eat. I'll look after to the horses.'

'Thanks. C'mon, Ray.'

CHAPTER TWELVE

'Come on in, folks.' Mrs Digby stood in the doorway to welcome them. She was a big and buxom young woman, with calloused hands and a sunburnt face. 'Make yourselves at home.'

The room into which the passengers went was dim and gloomy due to light coming from just one small window; the place having been built at a time when protection from attacks by Indians and outlaws was more of a consideration than comfort. And it was barely furnished, with benches either side of a long plank table. None of that mattered. What mattered was the stove blazing away in one corner.

Two large dogs, who were also relaxing in the warmth, eyed them warily but otherwise took no notice.

Greeley pushed Norton down onto the end of one bench. 'Sit there and keep quiet.' Then he joined everyone else at the stove. He hadn't realized quite how cold he was till then.

'Help yourselves to grub,' Mrs Digby went on. 'I baked the biscuits first thing this morning and the soup is good and hot. We were getting real anxious about you. It's real bad out there. What sort of journey have you had?'

Predictably it was Lewis who answered, telling her about the hazards on the trail; exaggerating them, too.

'Wish you could stay here longer 'til the storm passes over, but I just bet Bill'll want to be on his way soon as he can. He's a prideful man and likes to say he always keeps to the Wells Fargo timetable,' Mrs Digby smiled. 'You'll be safe enough with him. He's never had an accident all the years he's been coming this way. He'll get you through all right.'

'She must be very lonely don't you think?' Sarah said to Greeley as she took her place at the table by his side. 'Stuck out here on the edge of nowhere with just her husband and the dogs for company. No neighbours within miles. What happens if one of them takes ill?'

Greeley helped her and then himself to some of the biscuits and filled their bowls with the vegetable soup. 'From the look of her, I think Mrs Digby is the type of woman who takes everything in her stride and can deal with any sort of emergency. There are a lot of women like that who live on the frontier.'

His mother was one. She'd helped her eldest boy hold the family farm together, even after her husband's killing and one of her other sons leaving, against her wishes, to take on the precarious life of a bounty hunter.

'It's lonesome enough on the farm sometimes when we don't see anyone for days,' Sarah said with a little sigh. 'But at least we're not that far from Talbot and I have my family for company and support. Mrs Digby reminds me of Mary. She can cope with more or less anything, but all the

73

same I wish Tom hadn't taken her so far from us.'

Mrs Digby bustled around, making sure everyone had everything they needed, even Darren Norton, although otherwise she took no notice of him. Doubtless he wasn't the first outlaw in handcuffs that she had seen or fed.

Finally Greeley put down his spoon. 'Mrs Digby, that soup was delicious.'

'Thank you, dear, would you like some more?'

'Wouldn't say no.'

'What about you, dear?'

'Oh no I couldn't,' Sarah said. 'I'm quite full, thank you. Mr Greeley,' she added in a whisper as Mrs Digby began to dish out soup to those who wanted another bowlful, 'Mr Lewis keeps staring at me as if he suspects me of something. It's making me real uncomfortable.'

'I've noticed him looking at you too.' Greeley glanced across at the farmer. 'Would you like me to have words with him?'

'Oh no, I don't want to cause trouble or make things difficult for his wife. It's just that he seems to think he knows me from somewhere and is trying to decide one way or the other. But I've certainly never met him. How could I have? I've never been to Serenity before. And I don't think he believes I'm going there to visit with Mary, just because he doesn't know her and Tom.' She put a hand on Greeley's arm for a moment and raised her eyes to his. 'You believe me though, don't you? Please say you do.'

'Of course I do,' Greeley smiled. 'Why would you lie? How could Lewis possibly know all the people who live in and around Serenity? I bet you don't know all the farmers and their families near you in Talbot.'

'No, I don't.'

'He keeps staring at Anderson too. And you heard what his wife said. He believes he's met everyone before.'

'So she did.' Sarah sounded a little relieved. 'That's silly of him, isn't it?'

'Yes. Quite honestly I wouldn't take any notice of him. Lewis is a busybody and a bit of a nuisance, who wants to know everybody's business.'

Sarah drank the rest of her coffee, eyeing Lewis over the rim of the mug. 'I don't like him very much or the way he treats his poor wife, when she is such a nice kind lady.'

'She must be used to it by now and she doesn't seem to mind.'

'Or perhaps she doesn't have a choice.'

Brown stood up from where he and Daniels had been sitting at the far end of the table. He said, 'Stage is almost ready to leave, folks.'

'Anyone who wants to stay here can do so,' Mrs Digby said. 'We've got room and you're more than welcome.'

But despite the perils of the journey no one elected to remain behind, although Ruth looked as if she longed to suggest they do so to her husband.

Brown said, 'You've just got time to use the privy out back if you have the need.'

'I've made sure everything is nice and clean out there,' Mrs Digby said. 'Would you two ladies like to use it first?'

'Thank you,' Sarah said and left arm in arm with Ruth.

Almost as soon as the coach left the way station, it started the climb up into the hills. The road snaked round boulders and dense stands of trees and, as they got higher, crossed over high ridges to plunge down the other side of the hill before climbing again. It would be uncomfortable and slow going at the best of times and was now made much slower because of the constant rain and mud, the stage jolting them about as it slipped from side to side. Several times they almost came to a stop and Brown had to encourage the straining horses to get the stage moving again.

'We won't reach Serenity by Friday afternoon, will we?' Sarah said.

'No,' Greeley agreed. 'I doubt it.'

If the road got worse, they might not make it by Friday at all. They might have to spend two nights out on the open trail rather than one.

Thankfully, so far, they hadn't met any obstructions in the road and he didn't know what would happen or what they would do if they did. There was no other route through the hills as far as he was aware, at least not one suitable for a stagecoach. It might mean turning round and going all the way back to the way station.

'Look!' Sarah cried, pointing out of the window.

'Oh my!' Ruth added in a shocked voice. 'Oh, Clarence! See the river! Oh, it's awful.'

Normally at this time of the year the water would be sluggish, trickling over the white stones in the middle of the riverbed. Today it was a roaring and raging fury, pouring down the hill in high, wild waves and crashing into the banks in a never ending white foam, threatening to overspill them. It carried with it tree branches and rocks that tumbled helplessly this way and that in the rushing tide.

Everyone stared at it in horrified fascination. They were right to be scared for it was here that the accident happened.

CHAPTER THIRTEEN

Without warning the coach struck an unseen rock in the road. It rose high in the air and came down with a heavy bump, badly jolting the passengers. Across from Greeley, Lewis hit his head on the roof of the stage and Ruth almost fell off her seat, only staying upright by grabbing her husband's arm. As the wheels landed, they slipped in the mud and the coach threatened to topple over.

'Hell!' Greeley yelled. 'Hold tight!'

From above they could hear Bill Brown shouting encouragement and comfort to the frightened horses.

Even then Greeley thought they might be all right. The coach had righted itself. Brown was an experienced driver and just about had the animals under control.

And at that very moment the wheels hit a deep hole caused by the incessant rain. The coach rocked. The horses panicked. Brown pulled hard on the reins in an attempt to stop them. It was no use. The by-now terrified animals took off at a gallop. The coach was about to be involved in an accident. Nothing could prevent it.

With the wheels unable to get a purchase on the road's

slick surface, the coach slew around, this way and that. It careened hard into a tree, denting its side.

Amidst frightened screams and shouts, the helpless passengers were flung about in their seats. There was a jumble of arms and legs. This time Ruth did fall to land on top of Anderson. The guard was thrown from his seat.

The stagecoach slid along the road scraping against rocks and trees, whose branches were snapped off and whipped away, before suddenly its wheel hit a boulder with such force that it broke in two. Lopsided, the coach scraped along the ground for a few very long seconds, sparks flying out from underneath it, until its weight forced the horses to a halt. As they came to a shuddering stop, everything went quiet.

Greeley allowed time for his heart to stop its frantic beating before taking a deep breath. At least they were still on dry land and hadn't landed up in the river, where they would have been lost for sure.

'Everyone OK?' He was dismayed at the tremor in his voice.

He seemed to be almost at the bottom of a pile of bodies, with only Anderson beneath him. No one answered him and for a ghastly moment he was sure everyone else was either dead or badly injured. Then above him, Lewis shifted and managed to pull himself back up onto his sloping seat. And Greeley was suddenly aware of Ruth sobbing while Norton was swearing under his breath.

He sat up, holding his elbow, which he'd bashed hard, and said, 'It's all right. We've stopped now. Can we get out? It'll have to be on your side, Mr Lewis. We're stuck right up against a rock here.'

'I don't know. I'll try to open the door.'

'Where's the driver?' Ruth had panic in her voice. 'Help! Help!'

'Hush, Ruthie.'

'We're stuck in the middle of nowhere. Mr Brown is dead. I know he is. We'll never be found.'

Supposing Brown had been killed in the crash. If he, like the guard, had been flung from his seat he could have landed under the horses' hoofs, even beneath the stagecoach itself. And what had become of Daniels? Wisely Greeley didn't voice his fears. Instead he helped Ruth and Sarah to their seats, where they perched uncomfortably, trying not to slide off again.

Then he stood up as best he could and reached across Lewis to help him turn the door handle and push. At first nothing happened, but suddenly the door opened and fell backward with a bang. The stage rocked with the sudden movement and rain blew in soaking them within moments.

'Folks! Folks, you OK?' It was the driver, peering in on them. Brown was filthy dirty, covered in mud, and he had a bloody cut down one cheek. Otherwise he appeared unhurt.

'We're coming out,' Greeley said to Brown. 'I'll go first. Harry, can you help the others out after me? Don't worry, folks, me and Mr Brown will be here to catch you so you won't fall.'

The coach lay at an awkward angle, making it difficult to climb up to the door. There Greeley had to scramble through the opening and down the other side, reaching for Brown's hands as he did so. He landed in the mud and slipped to his knees.

'Steady,' Brown said.

'Lewis, come on, help your wife. Don't be scared, Mrs Lewis. There's a bit of a jump that's all.'

Ruth nodded bravely. The two men caught her as she slid down the side of the coach.

'Will you manage, Miss Fuller?' Greeley called up to her.

'Yes.' Sarah hitched up her skirt slightly, letting Greeley glimpse her shapely ankles. She climbed out of the stagecoach agilely, without the need for much help.

Lewis and Norton came next, followed by Anderson last of all.

Greeley was then able to look round and take stock.

Sarah and Ruth huddled close, arms around each other for comfort. The others were too stunned to do much more than stand where they were. Sarah's coat was torn along one sleeve and Norton had lost his hat somewhere. They were all mucky from the mud and rain and both Norton and Lewis had bruises and cuts on their faces and hands. Greeley doubted he looked any better. But while it didn't seem like they had much to be thankful for, they were alive when they could so easily have been killed.

Brown had cut the horses free from their harness before he'd come to find out how his passengers were. Now he went back to them and was stroking their necks and talking softly to them while they stood, shivering and agitated. They, like the passengers, looked unhurt.

Not so the coach. That clearly wasn't going anywhere any time soon.

'Mr Greeley, I'm sorry to be a nuisance, but can you get

my bag down?' Sarah said. 'It's got the clothes ma and me made for Mary's baby in it. I don't want to lose them.'

'In a minute.' Greeley didn't feel up to climbing onto the roof of the stagecoach. 'In fact it looks like we'll have to go on by foot and it might be best to leave our bags here. Carrying them will only slow us down. They can be retrieved later.'

'Oh no, please, I must have mine with me.' Tears came into Sarah's eyes. 'I can carry it myself. Please.'

'All right. I'll get it for you once we decide what to do. Don't worry.'

'Where's the guard?' Anderson suddenly asked.

'There!' Greeley pointed to where Daniels lay some way back along the road, attempting to sit up. He was perilously close to falling in the river. 'Quick!'

As Greeley and Anderson hurried towards him, Daniels sank back down, holding his arm. His face was covered in scratches.

'Is your arm broken?' Greeley asked as they reached him.

'Don't think so. It hurts like hell though. So does everything else. Get me up.'

Greeley caught him round the waist and helped him to his feet.

Daniels groaned then said, 'It's OK. I'm OK. That is . . . God! What a mess.' He'd just seen the coach. 'Hell, we ain't getting out of here on that, are we?'

'Nope.' Greeley shook his head. 'Let's go and see what Mr Brown has to say. Harry, stay with the others. Try to calm Ruth down.'

Brown grinned as the two men joined him. 'Hell, Ray,

you sure ain't had much luck on your first journey out here. You sure you ain't a jinx?'

'It ain't funny. I'm giving up this job and getting one that keeps me inside!'

'Mr Brown, can the horses be ridden? Can I take one and go for help?' Greeley eyed the animals doubtfully and wasn't surprised at Brown's answer.

'No, sir. They ain't riding horses and they're too het up to be handled safely right now. As for my coach, there's no way we can fix the poor old thing up. Far as I see it, there ain't no choice but for me to stay here with the horses and the stage, as they're my responsibility, while, Ray, you go on with the passengers and get 'em to safety.'

'Go on?' the guard echoed. 'Where to? Wouldn't it be best if we stayed together? Surely we'll be missed and someone'll come looking for us.'

'Not any time soon I'm afraid.'

'Mr Brown's right. We won't be missed in Serenity for a day or perhaps two and if there's any problems along the trail it might not be possible for anyone to come searching even then. It could mean a very long wait. And we need to get the ladies in the warm and dry. They've had a shock. The rest of us have too.'

'Yeah, I suppose you're right,' Daniels said. 'How far to the next way station?'

'No,' Brown said, 'that's way over yonder on the far side of the hills on the final run down into Serenity. It's too far for any of you to walk to, especially in this rain. 'Sides it's manned by just two young lads. They wouldn't know what to do.'

'What about back to the Digbys?' Then answering his

own question, Daniels said, 'No, that's miles back.'

'Do you have somewhere in mind?' Greeley asked, suspecting and hoping the driver did.

'You should make for the OP Ranch. The headquarters are only two or three miles off. In fact, iffen I have time I make a short stop there for coffee, although Wells Fargo don't need to know that, Mr Daniels, and I thank you not to tell 'em. Mr Peel is a good man, him and his wife will see you right. And he'll have men who'll come help me and my horses when they can.'

'How do we reach it?'

'That's the problem.' Brown scratched his chin. This was going to be bad. 'You follow the road for a mile or so and there's a ford across the river.'

Greeley and the other two men turned to look at the raging torrent. 'Hell!'

'It ain't usually a problem.'

'Well it will be now,' Greeley said. 'How will we get across? We won't.'

'Son, you ain't got a choice.'

Greeley considered all the possibilities and then nodded. It was either that or wait in the wet and the cold, without food or drink, maybe without the means to make a fire, for help to arrive and that could be days away. 'OK, we'll have to try it. Our bags can be left behind, although Miss Fuller wants hers. That'll make it a bit easier. C'mon, Mr Daniels, let's tell the others. Get going while there's still a bit of light. We want to reach the ranch before nightfall if possible.'

Which, just like being able to cross the ford, was doubtful.

Greeley wasn't in the least bit pleased. He'd caught the stagecoach to be safer in this storm and now look what had happened. 'Hell!'

CHAPTER FOURTEEN

'Well, there's the ford,' Daniels said.

Greeley's heart sank. It was worse than he'd feared.

The road ran down a steep slope to the river and, through the gloom, he could just about make out where it emerged on the other side and started up through a thick stand of pine trees. Normally the ford would be easy enough to cross, which was why the road was here. Not now. Rain continued to splash down on the torrent of water that spilled and churned and frothed between the two banks, almost overflowing. Even here, where the water level was at its lowest, it would still be at least knee high, made worse by the strong current.

They all stood in silence, surveying it fearfully.

'We can't cross it,' Ruth said in dismay, echoing all their thoughts. 'We'll drown. We'll have to go back.'

'We can't do that,' Daniels said. 'We'll just be stranded with the stage iffen we do. We have to go on.'

'I don't want to do this either,' Sarah said. 'Mr Greeley,

can't you and Mr Daniels go on to the ranch for help and leave us here?'

Greeley considered that, then said, 'The thing is, if we go together and help one another, and take it slowly, it looks like we can just about cross safely at the moment. But if the rain doesn't let up, and there's no sign of it doing so yet, and the water rises even higher that might not be possible. We could be stuck on the other side of the river and you could be stuck here for God knows how long, with no food or shelter.'

'How likely is that?'

'I don't know. It's a possibility is all. The other thing is you'll be alone with Norton. You don't want that, do you?'

'Oh no, not at all. I didn't think of that.' Sarah looked horrified. 'I'm sorry, Mr Greeley, you're right of course. I'll do my best. Don't worry about me.'

'What about the folks at the ranch?' Lewis said. 'Won't they send someone out looking for us?'

Greeley shook his head. 'Not yet. If at all.' When Lewis looked set to argue, he added, 'We can't depend on them. With the weather as it is, they might think the stage has been cancelled and likely they've got enough problems of their own without worrying about Wells Fargo. No, Mr Daniels is right. We must cross the river.'

There was no alternative. They had to reach the ranch.

Daniels pulled him to one side. 'It'll be best if I go first, see how deep it is in the middle and whether it is, actually, safe. If we all go together we risk everyone drowning. If it's OK, I'll come back and help you shepherd the others across. If it ain't, I'll go onto the ranch and seek their help.'

'You could be killed going on your own. Let me go with you.'

'As the stagecoach guard, it's my job to take the risks and I'll watch my step. And, Gus, iffen anything should happen to me, you'll be needed to look after the others and to make the decisions.'

'OK.' The plan was about the best in the circumstances.

'Hey, how about undoing these handcuffs?' Norton said when the rest were told. 'If I fall into that with them on I'll likely drown.'

'Nope, you can manage well enough. You're wanted dead or alive so it doesn't matter to me.' Right then Greeley didn't much care what happened to his prisoner. If it weren't for him, he wouldn't be out in this weather, wet through and in danger of drowning.

'Good luck, Mr Daniels,' Sarah said. She bit her lip. 'Be careful. Please.'

Daniels eased himself down the slope and stepped into the river. Arms out to each side he began to wade across, testing each step before he took it. Before long the water was up to his knees and in the middle it was even higher. There he was almost knocked over by a particularly strong wave. Sarah screamed and Greeley got ready to jump into the river to go to his aid. Somehow the guard righted himself. He paused for a moment to steady himself and then went on. Eventually he reached the far bank, where he stood, resting, head bent, hands on his knees.

Greeley said, 'You see. We can make it all right.'

'No,' Ruth said. 'I'm too frightened. I won't do it.'

'Yes you will.' Her husband patted her hand. 'I'll help you.'

88

'Let's go, folks,' Greeley said. 'We're all frightened but it'll be OK, Mrs Lewis. Just take it one step at a time. I'll go first and, Harry, you come last. We can keep an eye on everyone else and help anyone who needs it.'

'OK,' Anderson said a bit doubtfully.

Greeley repeated his earlier words of warning. 'And take it slow and carefully. Shall I take your bag, Miss Fuller?'

So far Sarah had insisted on carrying it herself and now she said, 'No, thank you. I can cope better than some of the others and you might need both hands free if anyone gets into difficulties.'

While Lewis took care of his wife with Anderson close behind, Greeley started down the mud-slick slope, Sarah close behind him. Norton looked after himself; no one was going to bother about him.

At the bottom Greeley waded into the water. He gasped. It was a tremendous, unexpected shock. Not only was the water freezing cold, it was furious. Endless waves bashed into his legs so hard he feared he would immediately lose his footing.

It was as if the river was alive. It wanted to knock him over, trap him and swallow him up. Underfoot the stones were treacherous, shifting about beneath his boots, trying to trip him up. He couldn't see through the spray and the rain. It was hard to catch his breath. Behind him he heard Sarah cry out.

He wasn't exactly sure what happened. They were more than halfway across and he was starting to think they would make it to safety without mishap when suddenly someone, and he didn't know who, fell against him.

Of course later on he realized exactly who was responsible and why, but at the time he thought it was just an unlucky and dangerous accident.

He lost his footing. Someone screamed. There were cries of horror. To his own horror, he found himself under the river, being dragged down. His body slammed into the riverbed. He couldn't stand up. Someone was pushing against him. The water pressed down on him, holding him fast. Trying not to panic, his feet scrabbled about until he found a purchase and he came up with a rush, gasping and choking, arms flailing, as he almost fell again. He seemed to have swallowed a lot of cold, dirty water and his eyes were stinging.

Close by Anderson, fear in his eyes, mouth open in shock and pain, tumbled against him. He went under, nearly pulling Greeley after him. Greeley grabbed for the young man's coat, jerking him upright. Anderson cried out and almost lost consciousness, becoming a dead weight in Greeley's arms. There were more cries.

'Hold on,' Greeley managed to say.

Seeing his difficulty, Daniels made an effort to get closer. After what seemed like a very long while he came near enough to catch hold of the drummer and steady him. Greeley now saw Sarah dragging Ruth along, the two of them having almost reached the other side.

'I'm OK,' Greeley gasped. 'Help the ladies out,' he said to Daniels. 'I'll see to Anderson. C'mon, Harry, it's not far to go now.'

At long, long last he reached the safety of the far bank. Pulling Anderson after him, he emerged from the river onto dry land, where he collapsed, gasping for breath, hardly able to believe he was out of the furious torrent and still alive. For several moments there he had believed he wouldn't make it.

'What the hell happened?' the guard asked, standing over him. 'One minute you were doing fine. The next you were in the water.'

Greeley shook his head wearily. 'Someone bashed into me and I went under.'

'You all did. I thought you were all going to drown.'

'So did I.' Greeley sat up and glanced round.

The others were out, collapsed on the bank, just like him. But something was wrong. .. . .

And at the same moment Ruth started to scream. 'Where's Clarence? Where's my husband? He's not here!'

CHAPTER FIFTEEN

'Oh my God!' Quickly Greeley looked round. Ruth was right. There was no sign of the farmer. Had he made it out of the river?

'Can you see him?' Daniels said.

'Who was with him?' Greeley asked at the same time.

'I think he was behind me,' Sarah said. 'But I lost sight of him when we all fell in the water. Afterwards I was occupied helping Mrs Lewis and I don't remember seeing him again.'

'Hell,' Daniels said. 'Perhaps he's come out further down.'

He hurried back to the river, looking this way and that, while Greeley waded back into the water by the ford, trying to spot the farmer. Anderson ran up and down the riverbank. They called out the man's name.

As for Norton, he leant against a tree, smirk on his face. Greeley longed to hit him or throw him into the river. Be done with him. $100 was hardly worth having to put up with the cocksure bastard.

Together Greeley and Daniels searched the river as best

they could. Then Daniels shook his head. It was hopeless.

'Any luck?' Greeley called to Anderson, who was some way away.

'No, no sign.'

Daniels said, 'It's no use, Gus, he's gone.'

And as much as he didn't like giving up the search Greeley had to admit the guard was right. The man must have been caught up in the river's swirl and his body could be miles away already. Together they struggled up the bank to where the others waited.

'You have anything to do with this?' Greeley snarled at Norton.

The young man shrugged insolently. 'No. How could I? In handcuffs?'

'Clarence? Have you found him?' Ruth cried as they joined her and Sarah, who was holding the woman close. 'Oh, where is he?'

Greeley put out a hand towards her. 'I'm real sorry, Mrs Lewis.'

The woman began to wail and Sarah held her even more tightly, one hand stroking her back.

'I'm sorry,' Greeley repeated. 'But we have to get on.'

'No, no, we can't leave him here all alone. He might be hurt and unable to call out for help. You must look for him again. Find him. Oh, please.'

'Can't you do anything more?' Sarah said.

'There's nothing more to be done,' Greeley told her. 'We daren't stay here any longer. It'll be dark soon and then our way will become even more treacherous than it is now.'

'Gus is right,' Daniels said. 'We can't do nothing for the poor guy.'

Sarah gave a quick nod to show she understood. 'Come along, Mrs Lewis. Let's find this ranch and get in the dry. Have something to eat and drink.'

'Oh, but I . . . oh, Clarence. Please. No, I'm not leaving him.'

'You must,' Greeley said. 'We'll come back later. Search for him then.' He knew it was an empty promise. Clarence Lewis had disappeared and was surely dead, his body lost forever. 'Let me take that for you.' He picked up Sarah's bag. For a moment it seemed she would object and he added, 'You stay with Mrs Lewis.'

Sarah nodded wordlessly.

Everyone was too exhausted for further talk. The only thing they wanted now was to reach the safety of the OP ranch.

Greeley feared they'd never get there.

He had no idea how far they trudged or what time it was. Time, along with everything else, ceased to matter. All that mattered was the ability to put one foot in front of another. For a long while there was no sign of the ranch. Perhaps it was much further away than Brown had thought. Perhaps they were heading in the wrong direction. Earlier Clarence Lewis had said he remembered the ranch from past journeys he and Ruth had taken to Talbot, but Greeley hadn't liked to ask Ruth which way to go; she was too distressed for that.

They'd have to come to a halt soon because before long it would be pitch-black and there could be any number of pitfalls on the road in front of them.

About the only good thing was that somewhere, some when, it stopped raining. At least if they were stranded in the open they might, with luck, find enough dry twigs to start a fire.

Then suddenly Anderson gave a cry. 'There! Look!'

And at the end of the valley, shining through the blackness, was the dim flickering light of several lamps.

'It must be the ranch,' Daniels said.

'I'll go on ahead and let the folks there know we're coming,' Greeley said. He already felt so much better at the thought of safety and warmth just a short way ahead of him that it was suddenly much easier to walk.

He reached a crossroads. The stagecoach road veered away from the ranch but another led in a straight line towards it. As he trudged closer, Greeley could make out a corral next to a bunkhouse and behind that several work buildings, while the ranch-house itself stood on a slight slope. One storey high, originally it must have been a simple two-room shack but it had been added to over the years so that there were now two wings and a veranda all the way along the front.

The lamps they'd seen had been lit by the bunkhouse and the barn and another shone by the door of the house. The ranch wasn't big enough to employ all that many men and those it did were probably out inspecting the damage caused by the storm. But someone must be home, for with blessed relief he also spotted the light of oil-lamps behind chinks in the shuttered windows of the house.

Weary and stumbling, he climbed up the porch steps and knocked on the door several times, desperate to be inside.

A few minutes later it was opened by a tall man with bushy brown hair and a drooping moustache. He held a rifle. Close behind him were two women.

'Who is it?' the elder asked.

'What d'you want, mister? What are you doing out on a night like this?' The man eyed him suspiciously.

Greeley gulped and in a croaky voice, said, 'Name's Gustavus Greeley. There's been an accident with the stage-coach.' He pointed back along the way he'd come. 'The passengers are on their way. Can you help us?'

'Oh my,' the woman cried. 'Orson, let him in. Quickly. You can see he poses no threat. The poor man is soaked through and he must be perished.'

Greeley stepped into light and dry and almost fell. He found himself in a large room that was used for both living and dining. There were wooden walls and floors and a lot of comfortable-looking furniture. Rag rugs were placed here and there. And best of all was a blazing fire. Heaven!

'How many passengers?' the man asked.

'Three other men. Two women. One lost her husband in the river.'

'Oh no!' That was the younger woman. 'How dreadful.'

'And I'm a bounty hunter and one of the men is my prisoner.'

Peel looked at his wife, unsure how she would react. He didn't look pleased himself. 'Betsy?'

'Don't worry, ma'am, I'll make certain he don't cause any problems.'

'He most certainly will not!' Mrs Peel was firm about that. 'I am not allowing someone who's done wrong having free rein in my house!'

For a dreadful moment, Greeley feared he and Norton would be turned away. He could hear the desperation in his voice as he said, 'Where can he go then?'

Peel thought for a moment. 'We can shut him in the root cellar. He'll be secure enough there. It can't be locked but we can put a table over the trapdoor leading to it. That way he won't be able to lift up the trap from below and get out.'

Betsy Peel nodded. 'That should be all right. It's dry down there and he can have a blanket to keep him warm. Now, Amelia, dear, don't just stand there. Put more wood on the fire. And start to boil up water so these people can have baths. And, Orson, you just go and help the other folks get here safely and quickly.'

'I'm on my way.' The rancher put down his rifle and reached for his hat and slicker. He picked up one of the oil lamps.

Greeley smiled: it was obvious who ruled the roost in the ranch-house.

'Come along, Mr Greeley, over to the fire. Let me take your hat and coat and you'd best take off your boots too. I'm Betsy Peel, by the way. That was my husband, Orson, and the girl is my daughter-in-law, Amelia. My son, Joseph, is out with the men looking after the cattle seeing what damage has been caused by this storm. They've been out most of the day and I'm expecting them back any minute now.' She bit her lip and stared towards the door, anxious that her son and the men with him should return in one piece. 'What happened? With the stage?'

Greeley told her as best as he could remember.

'Is Bill, Mr Brown, is he OK?'

'Yeah, he stayed with the coach and the horses.'

'He would,' Betsy agreed with a smile. 'He prefers

horses to people. And you say that someone died in the river?'

'Yes, ma'am, when we were crossing the ford. It was real treacherous and I'm not sure what happened exactly. He was a farmer by the name of Clarence Lewis. He comes from near Serenity. His wife is pretty shook up.'

'I can imagine. Well, don't you worry none. It's not your fault. Now, there's a stew on the go in the kitchen and there's plenty enough for everyone. Isn't that right?' she added to Amelia, who had just returned from the kitchen.

'It certainly is,' Amelia agreed with a little smile. 'We're used to dealing with emergencies out here.'

'Ah, here they are now.' Betsy turned as the door opened and, led by Peel, the others all tumbled in.

Ruth immediately sat down and began to cry. Betsy went over to her and sat beside her, holding her tight and speaking to her softly.

Meanwhile Peel pushed aside one of the rugs revealing the trap in the floor and pulled it open.

'Down you go,' Greeley said and gave Norton a shove.

'Ma, the water should be just about boiled,' Amelia said.

'Good. A hot bath for everyone. And then coffee and stew. In the meantime your outer clothes can be dried in front of the fire and I'm sure we can find some night-clothes for the ladies to wear later on. Mrs Lewis, perhaps you would like to go first? I'll come in and help you if you like.'

CHAPTER SIXTEEN

Greeley sank into the tin bath, set out in the room off the kitchen, and sighed in relief. The water had been heated up several times and was no longer all that hot or particularly clean. But he felt so much better, he might have been in the hottest, cleanest bath in the best hotel ever.

Dressed again in his damp clothes, he emerged into the main room, to find the place buzzing with people and activity. The passengers were sitting at the table eating stew and a place had been left for him beside Daniels. He took it gratefully while Betsy ladled meat and potatoes onto the plate.

The only one not eating much was Ruth Lewis. Her eyes were red-rimmed from crying and she looked as though she might start crying again at any minute. Greeley felt extremely sorry for her, losing her husband as suddenly as she had and having no body to bury. It was made worse because she was amongst strangers.

In the middle of the meal, Peel's son, Joseph, returned to the house along with the foreman, a gruff looking individual called Toby Williams. Betsy and Amelia started to fuss around them as well, glad they were back without mishap.

'So?' Peel said, after they'd both sat down. 'What's the damage?'

'Could be worse,' Joseph said. He gulped down some hot coffee before starting to report on the situation. He was about twenty-five and very much like his father. Waiting to be served with stew, he said, 'The cattle were spooked but they've calmed down now and aren't in any danger of stampeding. We lost two or three head but we got most of 'em on to higher ground before the storm really hit.'

'That's good. What about the land?'

Joseph frowned. 'Washed out in places and I reckon the river, especially higher up, will be impassable for some while.'

None of that sounded good; Greeley hoped it wouldn't delay for too long his departure with his prisoner.

Peel said, 'Tomorrow, so long as the weather don't get bad again, you and Toby can ride out and take a proper look round. And hopefully we can start bringing the cattle back down onto the lower pastures before long. Some of the men can try and get to Bill.' He gave his wife's hand a squeeze; he knew she was worried about the driver being left alone with nothing to eat or drink in the cold and wet. 'If there's no more rain the ford might be passable for horses by then.'

'I'll arrange all that,' Williams said.

Peel nodded. 'Meanwhile we should get some rest. It's been a long day.'

'Certainly has,' Daniels said. 'I'm exhausted. So is everyone else.'

Betsy smiled. 'There's a spare room and two beds where our four daughters used to sleep, which will do fine for Mrs Lewis and Sarah.'

'As for the rest of you there's room in the bunkhouse.'

'Actually, Mr Peel, iffen you don't mind I'd like to sleep in here,' Greeley said. 'Near my prisoner. I know he can't get out of the cellar and has nowhere to go if he does, but I want to be where I can keep an eye on him. I think Mrs Peel would feel better too if she knew someone was on guard.'

Betsy gave him a nod of agreement. 'I'll get you a pillow and blanket if you don't mind sleeping on the floor.'

'I've slept on far worse.' Greeley was so tired he didn't care where he slept so long as he could sleep somewhere.

'Talking of your prisoner,' Sarah said. 'I know he's done wrong an' all, but shouldn't he have something to eat? And a blanket to keep him warm?'

'All right,' Greeley said with a little laugh at her concern.

He poured out a mug of coffee and piled a plate with biscuits, while Betsy handed him a blanket. When he opened the trapdoor, Norton was sitting in a sulky heap at the bottom of the steps.

'Here, you've got Miss Fuller to thank for all of this.'

'Really?' Norton grinned.

As soon as the table was over the trapdoor again, Williams picked up an oil lamp. 'It's this way, folks.' He led Daniels and Anderson out into the cold night.

Greeley stood at the door, watching them go. Stars were blinking in the black sky and the air was full of the sound of the trees rustling and creaking in the still strong wind. The ground was thick with mud. But at least it didn't look like it was going to rain any more.

At last, Darren Norton thought sourly, they had remembered him! But had he been offered a bath or had his wet clothes taken away to be dried off? No! No one had bothered to suggest that. And here he was locked in the dark and stuffy root cellar, the only warmth coming from the room above him and the only light coming from cracks in the floorboards over his head. There was hardly any room for him to lie down and his pillow was a sack of potatoes. Mice scurried about in the walls.

Hell, life sure as hell wasn't fair. And with Serenity and the noose getting ever closer, that wasn't fair either and he was desperate to escape.

'Are you feeling any better, Mrs Lewis?' Sarah asked as she and Ruth prepared for bed.

Ruth shook her head and gulped. 'Oh dear, no, not at all. Oh, I can't believe I've lost Clarence. That he's gone and I'll never see him again. I know in some ways he wasn't that good a husband as he always wanted his own way, but he was *my* husband.'

'Had you been married long?'

'Yes, dear, we got married before the War. And mostly we rubbed along well enough together. And, oh, he was so happy about those pigs. It was to be the start of a new venture, one that he was sure would make us a healthy profit. Now I just don't know what will happen. What will I do without him?'

'Your son will be able to run the farm, won't he?'

'Yes, of course, but . . . oh dear . . . He doesn't know he's lost his father.' Ruth's voice faded away and she sank down on one of the beds, holding her head in her hands.

Sarah delved into her bag and brought out a bottle. 'Here, Mrs Lewis, have a slug of this. It's good brandy.'

'Oh no, dear, I couldn't. Clarence didn't approve of strong liquor.'

Sarah didn't say anything about him not being around any more. 'It'll make you feel better. Help you sleep. Think of it as medicinal. We've been through an awful lot today. What harm can it do? I'm most certainly going to have some.'

'All right then, dear, just a tad.'

Greeley lay down, wrapping the blanket round him. He planned to lie awake for a while making plans for how to get Norton down through the hills and into Serenity without any more difficulty, but as soon as his head touched the pillow he fell sound asleep.

CHAPTER SEVENTEEN

Greeley didn't wake up until Betsy Peel and Amelia got up to start breakfast. It was still dark outside. Life on a ranch, even for the owners, consisted of long hours. He dressed in a jacket that was still damp and boots that were wet and soggy, despite having been placed by the stove.

A little bit later the men wandered up from the bunkhouse at the same time that Sarah Fuller and Mrs Lewis began to lay out plates and mugs. From the kitchen came the smell of baking biscuits and frying bacon.

'Good morning, Miss Fuller,' Greeley said. 'Did you sleep well?'

'Yes, thank you.'

'You look cross,' he said, for the girl looked annoyed, quite unlike her usual self. 'Is anything the matter?'

'No, nothing.' The answer was short and sharp. Then Sarah put out a hand in apology. 'Oh I'm sorry, Mr Greeley, it's nothing truly, except for the situation we find ourselves in.'

At that moment Betsy and Amelia came in with jugs of coffee and plates laden with food.

'Orson! Jo!' Betsy called. 'Breakfast's ready. Sit down everyone. There's another long day ahead of us.'

'Will we be able to resume our journey today?' Sarah asked Greeley.

'I'd certainly like to try.'

Betsy paused in pouring out coffee for everyone. 'Oh no, you can't! You mustn't. It'll be much too dangerous. You heard what Jo and Toby said.'

Greeley looked out of the window. While it hadn't rained any more, deep puddles lay here and there and the wind was chilly and blowing hard. Grey clouds hung low in the sky, a mist forming over the looming hills. Betsy was probably right. Yet he didn't want to stay here, twiddling his thumbs, for who knew how long, waiting for help to arrive or the storm's damage to clear away. While he had no reason to doubt these people, they'd lived here a long time and were well versed in their surroundings and how the river behaved, perhaps, hopefully, it wouldn't be as bad as they feared: the land had a way of healing itself.

'Tell him, Orson. Make him see sense.'

'If you insist on going, I certainly can't spare anyone to go with you,' Peel said. 'My men are needed here to care for the animals and carry out repair work. Tell you what, just to satisfy my wife, why don't you wait for Jo and Toby to report back on what it's like. They can follow the river some way for you to see if it's passable lower down.'

Joseph added, 'It won't take us long, Gus. We'll be back

in time that, if it is OK, you should be able to reach Serenity before it gets dark.'

'All right.' That sounded like a sensible solution. 'I wouldn't risk it at all, ma'am,' he added to Betsy who looked worried, 'except that I want to hand Norton over to Marshal Rayner and get him locked up good and tight where he can't cause any more trouble. You want to be rid of him too, don't you?'

Betsy bit her lip. 'I have to confess I do.' She cast a nervous look at the trapdoor. 'I don't like having him in my house one bit. But I don't want it at the expense of you being hurt.'

'I won't take any unnecessary risks I can promise you that. And I won't go if Jo advises me not to.'

'When you leave, I'll go with you,' Daniels said. 'I can help you with your prisoner and while you deliver him to the jailhouse I'll let the Wells Fargo office know about the accident. They can send people out to deal with the stage-coach and the horses.'

'Be glad of the company.'

'That's settled then,' Peel said.

A short while later Joseph said, 'The men are already saddling up. I'll give 'em their orders and then me and Toby can get started too.' He gave Amelia a quick peck on the cheek and went out of the door.

'Orson,' Betsy called her husband back from following his son. 'I hope you're not thinking of going with them.' Her voice was stern.

Peel looked sheepish, caught out in his desire to ride with his men. He shook his head. 'No, all right, there's some damage to the corral fence. I'll make a start on fixing that.'

'Good.' Betsy stood up to begin clearing away the breakfast things at the same time as Sarah made a surprising request.

She said, 'Please, Mr Greeley, let me go with you as well.'

Betsy immediately sat down again. 'Oh no, you mustn't, my dear. If it's bad out there and there's an accident you could be badly hurt.'

'You'll only slow us down,' Daniels said.

'No, I won't. I'm a farm girl. I've been around horses all my life and I know how to ride. I won't hinder you, I promise. And I won't have an accident. Please. I must. Mary is due to give birth any day and I don't want to let her down. She needs me and expects me to be by her side.' Sarah turned pretty blue eyes on Greeley. 'Please. It's so important to me.'

'I'm sorry. I can't chance you either being hurt or being used by Norton as a means of escape. I can't be responsible for him at the same time as looking out for you.'

'I can take care of myself.'

'No, I'm sorry. But I promise that as soon as I get to Serenity I'll find someone to take a message to your sister's farm and tell her what's happened. She'll know it's not your fault if you don't reach her in time.'

'That'll be for the best,' Betsy said. 'Don't fret, dear. I'm sure your sister will understand. And it won't be long before you can join her. This weather will soon clear.'

'Oh all right.' Sarah didn't look very pleased. 'If you both think you know what's best for me.'

Betsy was surprised at the girl's angry and mutinous

tone. 'I'm sorry, dear, we're only thinking of you and your safety.'

'I know and I'm the one who should apologize for being ungracious.' Sarah smiled.

Betsy got to her feet again and turned to her daughter-in-law. 'Come on, Amelia, there's women's work to be done. I know it's not washday but with all the rain and all these extra people, there's an awful lot of wet and dirty clothes and towels in the laundry. Too many to leave. Luckily it's a good drying day. We'll get started as soon as we've washed up.'

'You must let Miss Fuller and me help you,' Ruth said. 'I shall be glad of something to do to take my mind off my poor dear Clarence.'

'Thank you, my dear. We'll be glad of your help.'

'Mrs Lewis, perhaps you'll help me sweep the floor and put the chairs away,' Sarah said, having recovered her good nature. 'Then we can all set to with the laundry. Mr Greeley, why don't you carry some of the heavy plates out to the kitchen for Mrs Peel.'

'All right.' Greeley didn't mind being bossed around by a pretty young lady.

When he went into the kitchen, Betsy said, 'Just put the dishes down there, Mr Greeley. They need to be soaked. And, Amelia, fetch me . . .'

She got no further.

From the direction of the parlour came the sound of a gunshot, followed by a scream, a thump and quickly another scream.

Startled, Betsy dropped the plate she was holding on the floor and it smashed to pieces. She looked at

Greeley, fear in her eyes.

What now?

What the hell was happening?

CHAPTER EIGHTEEN

Several thoughts tumbled round in Greeley's mind even as he ran back to the parlour, Betsy and Amelia close on his heels.

He'd been right to be suspicious of Harry Anderson. The young man was a friend of Norton's and had caught the stagecoach to help him escape. Or maybe it was Ray Daniels, the new guard that Brown had never met before.

One of them had shot someone while helping Norton escape from the root cellar. Or someone had shot one of them to prevent a rescue. They were all unlikely but none of them was nearly as unlikely as the shocking scene that greeted him.

'Oh my!' Betsy gasped behind him.

Daniels lay on his back in the middle of the floor, unmoving, his shirtfront already stained with blood, while Anderson stood by the table rigid with surprise.

And there, back to the wall, was Sarah Fuller, smiling and holding a gun. She was also holding a terrified Ruth in front of her, pressing the gun barrel deep into the woman's neck.

Betsy immediately went to help Daniels and Sarah said, 'No, leave him.'

'But I must . . .'

'Ma, don't.' Amelia caught hold of her mother-in-law's arm. She had seen the look in Sarah's eyes.

The door opened and Peel rushed in. 'What is it? My God!'

'Come on in,' Sarah said. 'Shut the door. And shut up. All of you stand over there by the table with Harry and don't try anything stupid or say anything stupid either, else I'll shoot poor Mrs Lewis, which I really don't want to do.'

'Best do as she says,' Greeley said when finally he found his voice. He'd seen her eyes too and felt sure she meant exactly what she said.

Peel took no notice. Perhaps he couldn't believe Sarah was capable of what she threatened. 'Give me the gun, Miss Fuller,' he said. 'There's no need to hurt anyone else.'

Before Greeley could stop him, the man took a couple of steps towards the girl.

Without hesitating, she turned the gun on him and fired, hitting him in the leg. With a cry of pain he fell to the floor.

'Orson!'

'Pa!'

Nothing and no one could have stopped the Peel women as they rushed to his side. Betsy dropped to her knees, cradling his head, murmuring his name, while Amelia quickly tore a strip from her petticoat to bind the wound.

'How touching.' Sarah seemed to find their concern funny.

111

This was a different Sarah. No longer the naïve and pleasant farm girl. But someone hard and quite ruthless.

Greeley's heart thumped loudly as he demanded, 'What the hell do you think you're doing?'

'What does it look like?'

'You're going to rescue Norton.'

'Spot on.'

'But why?'

'Work it out.'

'You're involved with him, of course.'

'Clever boy,' Sarah laughed. 'Right again.'

Greeley cursed. He hadn't once suspected that they even knew one another, let alone anything more. Not once had they acknowledged each other by word or deed and Sarah's act of being scared of the young man had been convincing. While he'd ignored her completely.

'Naturally you, like everyone else, never realized he was my lover. We both played our parts too well for that. Now we're going places together and no one is going to stop me. Does that shock you, Gustavus dear? You might find it even more shocking to learn that I'm a whore.' Sarah laughed at Betsy's gasp. 'That's right, Mrs Peel, I've been one for years. They call me Sal the Gal. Actually, although I like the life, I'm hoping to give up that occupation quite soon and open a brothel of my own in San Francisco. With Darren. Pity, Gustavus, that you won't be one of my first customers. I quite like the look of you.'

Greeley had once liked the look of her too.

Sal laughed again. 'Your faces! You're all oh so respectable, ain't you? And now you know what I am, you consider me a nobody. Well, let me tell me I'm soon going to have more money than the rest of you put together. I shall become quite the lady. Own a horse and carriage and have servants of my own. What do you decent folks have to say to that?'

Ruth cried out as Sal pressed the gun harder into her flesh.

'Don't,' Greeley said. 'She hasn't done anything to you.'

'Oh do be quiet. Instead of babbling away, make yourself useful. Push back the table and let Darren out of the root cellar.'

'Please do as she says,' Betsy begged, wiping tears from her eyes. 'We don't want Mrs Lewis to be hurt.'

At which Ruth gave a little whimper of fright and pain.

With little choice but to do as Sarah, no Sal, ordered, Greeley indicated to Anderson that they move the table. As he did so, he glanced at Daniels, unable to tell if the man was still alive or not. Thankfully Peel didn't seem badly hurt. He was white-faced with pain and shock, but was sitting up, leaning against his wife's knees. When Greeley pulled open the trapdoor, he saw Norton on his feet, looking up expectantly; he must have heard the shots and some at least of what was said.

Pulling Ruth with her, Sal went up to the opening. 'Hi there, Darren. Come on up, darling. We ain't got all day.' She grinned at his expression of delight.

'Sal!' he cried. He started up the steps and groaned. 'My legs are numb from being down here for so long.'

'Never mind that, just get on up here.' When Darren joined her, Sal gave him a quick kiss and then said. 'Get Peel's gun. And, Gustavus, perhaps you'd like to remove your pistol from its holster and place it, CAREFULLY, on the floor.'

Reluctantly he did as she ordered. And Norton picked it up, holding it awkwardly because he was still handcuffed.

'Good. Now, all of you, get on down into the root cellar.'

'That's the thing, Sal! Let them suffer like they done made me. It was cold and dark down there. They didn't care nothing about me.'

'We fed you . . .' Betsy began before her husband nudged her to keep quiet.

'Anyone got any objections?' Sal mocked. 'No, I didn't think so. You should be grateful I don't shoot you all as well. Go on, quickly! Oh, don't bother about the guard. Leave him lying where he is and, Gustavus, not you. You wait up here with me.'

Betsy gave him a startled look.

'It's all right,' Greeley said, although he doubted it was, especially when Sal laughed.

Betsy and Amelia helped Peel down the steps into the cellar, with Anderson following close behind.

'You too.' Sal gave Ruth a hard shove so that she almost fell.

Greeley caught her arm and helped the trembling woman follow the others. 'She won't hurt you now,' he said to reassure her and she nodded gratefully.

'Now, Gustavus dear, shut the trapdoor and move the table on top of it so they can't get out. Good.'

'What about these?' Norton held up his handcuffed wrists.

114

'Give me the keys,' Sal ordered Greeley.

As she held out a hand, he considered going for his gun and making a stand. He dismissed the idea just as quickly. There were two guns held on him now and he didn't doubt that both Norton and Sal would use them. Sal had shown herself quite willing to fire a gun and Norton had nothing to lose. Best to submit now and hope to seize a better chance later on.

That was if there was a later on for him, which he wasn't at all sure there would be. Sal looked capable of anything.

'Hurry it up,' she said with a glance out of the window.

'Here you are.' Greeley gave her the key, scowling at Norton even while Norton smirked back.

'Handcuff him in my place. See how he likes it. Stop him getting any ideas.'

With her own smirk, Sal did so and then tossed the key into the far corner of the room. Turning she picked up her bag that she'd placed by the door and said, 'Now, for chris'sakes, let's get on down to the barn and, Gustavus dear, you can come with us. Then me and Darren will be on our way. Walk ahead of us.'

'You won't get away with this, you know.'

'Don't see why not. I usually get away with most every-thing I do. Even killing that stupid farmer. None of you so much as suspected me of any foul play. You thought it was an accident.' Sal smiled. 'It was easy. I just bided my time and then amid all the confusion at the ford, which I caused by the way by falling against you, Gustavus dear, I knifed him and held him under the water till he drowned.'

Greeley was horrified at her boasting and he was

amused to see that Norton didn't look all that happy either.

'Almost drowned you too when you went under. But I decided you could still be useful at some point.'

'What had Lewis done to you?'

'He said he recognized me.'

'You knew damn well he said that to everyone. He didn't mean it.'

'I know. It's a shame, isn't it? But I couldn't take any chances. Iffen you had learned I worked in a cathouse you'd've suspected me straight off of being involved with Darren. Besides I didn't like Mr Lewis and the way he kept on and on and on. And as for the way he treated his poor wife and how he spoke to her was just plain horrible. And wrong. I did her a favour. She's better off without him. Like my ma was better off without her husband though she never admitted it.'

For a fleeting moment Sal looked quite sad, but the look was gone so quickly Greeley wondered if he'd imagined it.

By now they had reached the barn.

'Those two horses there, Gustavus dear, they look steady enough. That is one thing I told the truth about. I did grow up on a farm and I've been around horses all my life. Fetch them for us. And be quick about it. I don't want any of the cowboys coming back and catching us before we can be on our way. I haven't done all this and risked my life to be stopped by a bunch of hicks.'

Greeley turned to the horses. As he did so, he heard movement close behind him. There was Darren's snigger, followed by Sal's giggle. Before he could do anything, Sal

116

brought the barrel of her gun down as hard as she could on his head. Stars burst before his eyes and he collapsed to the ground with barely a sound.

CHAPTER NINETEEN

Early in the morning, Marshal Rayner spent time walking round Serenity, inspecting people and the town.

The storm had caused a lot of damage, with some flooding, serious in places, while several fences and walls had been knocked down by the wind. Holes had appeared in the streets and mud and debris piled up under the sidewalks. A few people were hurt, some with broken limbs, and a couple of men had almost drowned. Thankfully there had been no fatalities.

And now at last the sun was breaking through the clouds, warming everything up and drying it out. Stores were reopening. The saloons had never closed, despite Rayner's warnings. It would be soon be business as usual.

On the way back to his office he called in on Greg Morgan. The telegraph operator didn't look pleased to see him, nor pleased with life in general.

'Telegraph is still out,' he said abruptly. 'So, no, there ain't been a reply from Wells Fargo about who was or wasn't on the damn stage. And, no, there ain't been a reply from Talbot about Judge Quinn. You'll just have to wait like everyone else.'

'OK,' Rayner said. 'Let me know as soon as it's back in action.' And he left Morgan to stew in whatever was wrong. It was probably something to do with that sour-faced wife of his.

Earlier he'd sent Frank Evans out to look at the river and he didn't have long to wait before his deputy returned from the ride. Evans looked cold and miserable. As he took off his hat and hung up his coat, Rayner poured them both out coffee.

'Well?'

Evans shook his head. 'It's still awful out there. And, Charley, the bridge is well and truly down. The stage hasn't a hope of getting through.'

'Hell!' Rayner looked shocked. 'Are you sure?'

'There ain't much of it left, except for some of the structure on both banks and a few posts in the river. The rest has been washed clear away. And the river is running higher and faster than I've ever seen it. There's no way the stage can be driven through it, not like it is at the moment. It'd overturn or get stuck for sure. I doubt even a rider could get across.'

'Hell,' Rayner said again. He thought for a moment. 'Well, if the stagecoach driver knows his stuff, and Bill Brown surely does, he could go a couple of miles out of his way to where there's a crossing lower down.' He frowned. 'But even Bill might not want to do that when he'd have no guarantee the river'll be passable even there.'

'I didn't ride that far to see.'

'Didn't expect you to.' Rayner sighed. 'I'm guessing we won't be able to set about repairing the bridge just yet.'

'Not till the river goes down.'

'All the same you might start rounding up those men who'll be willing to help in the rebuilding. Tell 'em they'll be paid out of town funds. I know there are a lot of things here in Serenity need repair too, but the bridge is our priority. It's our lifeline to Talbot and elsewhere.'

'OK.' Evans nodded. 'There won't be any shortage of volunteers. Everyone knows how important it is. What will you be doing?'

'I'll have to tell Artie what's going on. He's expecting the stage to arrive sometime today with Norton on it.' Rayner shrugged. 'Whereas we don't even know if Greeley and his prisoner managed to catch it. And, even if they did, it's obvious it's going to be a while yet before they can get here.'

'Can't help the weather.'

'After that I'll ride round some of the farms, see if any of 'em need help. And on the way back I'll take a look at the river for myself.' He glanced out of the window. Perhaps with the improvement in the weather, things would start to get back to normal quite quickly, although that was probably a forlorn hope.

'Charley, is it OK if I ride out to Irene's place? Make sure she and her folks are all right?'

'Yeah, 'course. Artie will want to know about them as well.' Putting on his jacket, Rayner paused as he got to the door. 'By the way, Frank, you see any sign of Sal the Gal out there?'

'No, sir, nary a one.'

'Pity.' Rayner sighed again.

He reckoned Sal was either dead or lying somewhere

badly injured. Maybe she'd drowned in the river. He doubted they'd ever know for sure.

'Ain't much of a let up yet,' Toby Williams said after he and Joseph had ridden a little way down the hillside, following the course of the river, which still showed little sign of abating. 'The bounty hunter'll have his work cut out iffen he insists on making the journey to Serenity today, especially if he comes this way. Reckon his best bet will be to make a long detour and come out further down the valley. Take him longer though. If he had any sense he'd leave it for a day or two, but I doubt he will.'

'It is slightly better than yesterday,' Joseph pointed out. 'So maybe he'll be OK. He seems pretty experienced. Up to him anyhow. Hopefully it's better at the ford and the men will be able to get to Bill and the horses.'

'One thing, Jo, we ain't seen no sign of any stranded or dead cattle.' The livestock was what the foreman was mostly worried about.

'No . . . wait up, Toby, what's that?' Joseph pointed at the riverbank. 'There see.'

Something was caught up amongst the rocks and rushes on this side of the river. Something bulky, that shouldn't be there.

'I'll go see.' Williams dismounted.

Pushing back his slicker so that if need be he could get at his gun, he made his way to the edge of the bank, careful not to slip in the mud. His heart skipped a beat as he realized that it wasn't a dead animal but a man's body. Some poor soul who had got caught out in the storm and landed up in the river. Thankfully not one of the OP men:

they were all accounted for.

Joseph joined him. 'Hell. It must be that passenger from the stagecoach. If he was lost at the ford, the tide could easily have carried him all the way down here. Let's get him out.'

Williams braced himself against the bank and reached down for the body. Joseph held on to his legs to stop him from falling in as he grabbed the dead man's jacket.

Williams heaved. The body was stuck in the rushes somehow, but after a moment it came free with a horrible sucking sound. He fell backwards, pulling the corpse after him. Scrambling to his feet, he and Joseph dragged it to the top of the bank and there turned it over on to its back.

Joseph swore. 'What the hell is that?'

The man hadn't drowned as everyone had naturally assumed. He'd been stabbed in the throat, leaving behind a large, gaping wound.

Murdered!

'Who did this, Toby? Indians?' Joseph looked nervously at the surrounding trees.

Williams shook his head. 'Can't be. They wouldn't've been out yesterday. They'd've had more sense. 'Sides we ain't had Indian trouble in the hills for years. They don't stab their victims neither. And the other passengers didn't report seeing any sign of Indians or anyone else either.'

'They believed Lewis was drowned. How could he have been stabbed without them seeing that either?' Joseph pushed his hat to the back of his head and frowned, trying to puzzle it out. 'So was he drowned first at the ford and then stabbed later by someone who wasn't on the stage? No,' he answered his own question, 'that makes even less sense than an Indian attack.'

'None of it adds up. But, Jo, this man has been stabbed and, think about it, it must have been at the ford. By someone who was clever enough to fool the others into thinking his loss was an accident. But why? Why was he, a farmer, killed, when none of them had met him before?'

'Or at least said they hadn't.' The two men looked at one another and Joseph went on, 'It must be to do with Norton.'

'He couldn't have stabbed anyone,' Williams objected. 'He was in handcuffs and that bounty hunter, who surely don't look like anyone's fool, would've searched him for weapons.'

'Perhaps he had an accomplice on the stage who had some reason of his own to murder Lewis.'

'Well if so, and whatever the truth of the matter, whoever did this is back at the ranch-house with your family.'

Joseph's face whitened. 'We've got to get back there quick. Warn them.'

Williams was already picking up the corpse. He carried it up to where the two horses waited. He threw it unceremoniously over the back of his horse and mounted behind it.

'Come on, there's no time to lose.' Joseph spurred away.

Williams followed. He had an awful feeling that they were already too late. If anything had happened to the Peels. . . .

CHAPTER TWENTY

Sal laughed and kicked out at Greeley's inert body.

Norton laughed too, but the look of awe he gave the girl was tinged with slight feelings of disquiet. Then she kissed him long and hard. And he forgot everything except how exciting it was to be with her. She was exciting.

'You're a wonder,' he said, meaning it. 'Has anyone ever told you so?'

'They don't call me Sal the Gal for nothing!'

'Let's get outta here.' Norton went over to one of the horses. 'What's the plan, Sal?' She must have one.

'Wait a minute.' Sal stopped him. 'What about him?' She kicked Greeley again.

'What about him?'

Sal sighed. Sometimes Darren could be so stupid. 'Don't you want to shoot him?' She fingered the gun she'd stuck in the belt of her skirt. 'You'd like to see him dead, wouldn't you, after the terrible way he treated you?'

For a moment Norton thought, yes, the bastard deserved to be killed for what he'd done. But it was one thing to fantasize about shooting Greeley, and the others too, what with the way they looked at him and talked about looking forward to seeing him hang, and quite another to actually do it in cold blood, especially when Greeley was lying unconscious and helpless at his feet.

Norton had shot Arthur Hamlin in a fit of temper, giving the young man no chance to defend himself and he'd regretted it ever since, although he wouldn't admit that to Sal, who would probably see it as a sign of weakness. That had been the start of his troubles and he didn't want to commit another murder.

And deep down he felt horrified that Sal would suggest such a thing seemingly without any qualms. Even worse, she'd killed the farmer just in case he recognized her, when she must have realized he was simply a braggart, who couldn't possibly know her. No two ways about it, Sal the Gal was an unrepentant murderess.

'No.' He caught her arm.

'No? Why not? You ain't turning soft on me, are you, Darren?'

'Like you said, some of the cowboys might be back at any moment and I'd rather get away than dilly-dally around getting my revenge and perhaps be caught.' That was as good an excuse as any.

Sal eyed him doubtfully. 'It wouldn't take but a minute to shoot him.'

Hell! Norton thought desperately and said, 'But if any of the men are nearby and they hear a shot they'll come running and come after us. We're wasting time, arguing. Let's go. Anyway it'll hurt Greeley's pride to know I've gotten away from him and that he's lost his bounty on me. And, even worse, that he's been bested by a girl.

That'll be punishment enough.'

'Oh all right,' Sal said with a sulky sigh.

Thank God she agreed with him because Norton hadn't known what he would do otherwise; whether he'd be able to stop her. Or whether she'd turn on him if he tried.

As they rode away, Sal regained her high spirits.

So did Norton who said, 'I couldn't believe my eyes when you walked into the stage office in Talbot. I nearly fell off my chair in surprise.'

'Good job you didn't. You'd've given the game away. You played your part same as me. No one had the least idea we knew one another.'

'You even managed to fool Greeley.'

Sal smiled. 'That was oh so easy. You just have to have a pretty face and a helpless air. And Greeley was too busy looking at my ankles to notice anything else. The only one who was suspicious of me was that fool of a farmer and I made sure no one listened to him.' She leant across to stroke Darren's arm. For some reason, although he was trying to hide it from her, he looked unhappy that Lewis was dead. 'I'm real sorry I had to kill him.'

Although she wasn't, not really. He'd just been another man, in a long line of men, who thought himself so much better than women and who had treated his long-suffering wife as if she was of no account with no thoughts or wants of her own; putting himself first in everything. Maybe he didn't deserve to die over the remote possibility he guessed who she was, but at the same time she wasn't about to harbour any regrets over what she'd done.

Darren seemed satisfied by what she said.

126

'How did you get to Talbot in the first place?'

Quickly Sal told him about robbing Queenie, which made him roar with laughter. Serve the old bitch right!

'When I left Serenity, I took the long way round to Talbot.' Even Sal hadn't dared ride the horse up through the hills by herself, even though that would have been quicker. 'I thought I'd've more time than I did, but the wind slowed me down and it was a tough journey. I was scared I wouldn't make it in time but I did, didn't I?'

'You're a wonder,' Norton repeated. 'I certainly wouldn't've liked to make that journey by myself, at night, with the storm brewing. You're real brave.'

Sal grinned. It was nice to bask in a man's adoration. 'I set out to do something, I do it.'

'Where are we going, Sal?'

'California, of course! San Francisco. I've got Queenie's money in here.' She patted the bag slung over the saddle-horn. 'I stole more than enough to start up my own brothel. Just think of it!'

Even so, despite her boasting, Sal was annoyed with herself. Her first idea had been to get up in the night when everyone else was in bed. She could then knife Greeley while he was asleep and rescue Darren and they could ride away with no one being any the wiser and they would be miles away before anyone could come after them.

But she'd had a couple of brandies along with Ruth, because even she'd been scared by the storm and found the going dangerous and frightening. While waiting for the other woman to fall into a drunken stupor, she'd pretended to go to bed. There, in a rare moment of weakness, she'd fallen asleep herself. And hadn't woken till dawn crept in the window, by which time it was too late to put her plan into action.

No wonder Greeley thought she looked cross; she was!

Then Greeley had come up with the plan of taking Norton back to Serenity and agreed that Daniels could go with him. On the trail she would have found the chance to get Darren away from the two men, but the bastard had had the gall to refuse to allow her to go along.

Instead she'd had to think fast about what to do and then wait to act until all the hands had left the ranch and just the family and the stagecoach passengers were present.

She knew there wouldn't be long before some of the men came back. She also knew she was taking a risk to go up against them all; she might have been overpowered, but she'd had no choice. In the event they'd been taken by surprise and no one had stopped her.

She'd soon be in California: San Francisco. Where there was so much gold and men willing to spend it! Never again would she have to be that silly, simpering Sarah, the farm girl she once was and who she'd left behind years ago. As she had left behind that hated life and her hated father.

She could once more and always forever be Sal the Gal.

Whooeee!

CHAPTER
TWENTY-ONE

Slowly Greeley opened his eyes. And groaned. His head felt like it was about to burst. He felt sick. Raising a hand towards his head, he realized he was wearing handcuffs. Then he realized why. So, however much he wanted to, he couldn't lay where he was forever. After a moment or two he forced himself to sit up, groaning again as he did so.

There was, of course, no sign of Norton or Sal or the two horses. They could be anywhere by now, especially as he had no idea of how long he'd been knocked out cold. Neither did he have any idea of why he was still alive. Why he hadn't been killed.

Another groan, this time at his own stupidity. He couldn't believe Sarah Fuller had made such a dupe of him. He'd been completely taken in by her blue eyes and trim waist. Believed in her innocent act and believed all her lies. Never once suspected she was other than what she said. It hardly helped that everyone else had been fooled by her too. Norton had played his part; he'd been fooled by him as well.

Yet it made sense that she and Norton were involved. It was likely that a young man such as he was would want to enjoy the favours of a pretty young lady and likely that a young lady, who earned her living in a brothel, would be attracted to his wild ways and handsome face.

Greeley closed his eyes, gritted his teeth and managed to stand upright on wobbly legs. He almost fell but grabbed at a post and held on until the barn stopped its awful whirling round.

He made it out into the yard just as Joseph Peel and Toby Williams galloped into view. Williams had a body slung over the saddle in front of him. Clarence Lewis, the farmer, it had to be. Greeley raised a hand and they rode up to him.

'What's happened?' Joseph cried, flinging himself off his horse. 'Are my family all right? What's going on? We found that farmer you were talking about. Is anyone hurt?'

'Sarah Fuller was Norton's girlfriend. She's shot your pa and Daniels. And she hit me hard. That's the last thing I remember.'

Joseph swore and immediately raced for the house.

'Don't worry,' Greeley called after him. 'They're safe in the root cellar.' Holding his head he turned to Williams and quickly added, 'Peel isn't badly hurt. I'm not sure about Daniels.'

'What a mess,' Williams growled.

It was obvious that the foreman didn't appreciate the fact that Peel and Betsy had taken the stagecoach passengers in, dried them off and fed them, only to be repaid by having danger and murder brought to their door. Who could blame him? Greeley didn't like it either.

'Your head's bleeding,' Williams said, catching hold of Greeley as he stumbled. 'And you're in handcuffs,' he added with a grin.

Greeley groaned again, this time at the humiliation.

'They can't have gone long. We came back as soon as we found this poor guy.' So saying, Williams lifted Lewis's body off the horse and carried it into the barn. 'Let's get you up to the house.' He put an arm round Greeley's waist in support.

By the time they got there, Joseph had let the prisoners out of the root cellar. They looked angry and fearful, not really understanding what had happened.

Greeley was relieved to see that he was right about Peel: the rancher wasn't badly hurt. The bandage Amelia had made from her petticoat and wrapped round his leg was barely stained with blood and he sat in a chair, cursing and muttering.

Not so Daniels. He lay on the floor and Betsy and Amelia were both by his side. They had cut away his shirt and now Betsy said, 'Amelia, dear, boil up some water. We'll have to bathe this wound and bandage him up good and tight. I don't think I can get the bullet out. It's too deep for me to risk it.'

'She has operated on others in the past,' Williams said in an aside to Greeley. 'But that was mostly for flesh wounds or broken limbs. Let's get you out of the hand-cuffs. Where's the key?'

'Sarah threw it into the corner. Over there.'

'Here we are.' Williams freed him.

'Jo,' Betsy said, 'help me carry Mr Daniels into the

bedroom. Let's get him settled.'

'Mrs Lewis,' Greeley said, turning to the woman, who had collapsed into a nearby chair and was twisting a handkerchief round and round in her hands. She raised scared, tearful eyes to him. 'I'm so sorry, but they've found the body of your husband.'

'Oh no, no. Oh, I hoped . . . oh, poor Clarence. I must go to him.'

'He's in the barn.' Greeley turned to Anderson. 'Go with her.'

'Come along, Mrs Lewis,' Harry said and, holding her arm, took her out of the door.

Peel ran a hand through his hair. 'I was real worried about you, Gus. We all were. Thought you'd be dead for sure.'

'Me too,' Greeley said with a little laugh. 'Got knocked out is all.'

'I can see that.'

Greeley put a hand to his head, feeling a large bump at the back of his neck. As he touched it, he winced and a wave of nausea surged through him. He swallowed hard. He sat down before he fell down. That was a bit better.

'Gus, I'm real angry about all this. . . .'

'You have every right to be.'

'. . . but none of it is your fault.'

Greeley shook his head and wished he hadn't. 'Yeah it is. I should have been suspicious of everyone on that stage. Not allowed myself to be hoodwinked.'

'You couldn't've known. That girl was a complete law unto herself.' Peel sighed. 'She sure put on a show.'

'I should get after them.'

'No.' Peel held out a hand. 'Not till you're feeling better. You try riding off now, you won't get far. I want that pair caught same as you after all they've done, but you won't catch 'em if you fall off your horse and can't get on again. You need to rest a bit. Have something to eat. Soup won't take long to heat up. An hour or two won't make much difference either way.'

Reluctantly Greeley accepted what the man said. He really didn't feel up to a long ride just yet. 'I'll go as soon as I can.'

'Doubt you'll catch up with 'em,' Williams said.

'But at the least I need to alert Marshal Rayner. And a doctor is needed out here to look at Daniels and you too, Mr Peel.'

'In which case iffen it's OK with you, sir, I'll ride down into Serenity with Gus,' Williams said. 'He doesn't know the way whereas I do. That way he can stay in Serenity while I bring the doc back with me.' The way he spoke he wouldn't take no for an answer from either Greeley or the doctor.

'Good idea,' Peel agreed.

A little later Betsy came back into the room. 'Daniels is sleeping easily,' she said. 'He's still losing blood though.' She went up to her husband and put her arms round him, holding him close. 'I don't think anything vital has been hit. He'd be dead by now if it had. And the fact that he's still alive is a good sign. Oh, Orson.'

Betsy began to cry.

'It's all right,' he said, patting her arm. 'I'm OK. I've been hurt worse, you know that. It's over now. You've had more to cope with than this.'

She gulped. 'It was just such a shock. That girl! All she did. What she was. To think we trusted her. Liked her even. I can't get over it.' After a moment or two she sat up straight and wiped her eyes. On a ranch there was never much time for weeping; you had to get on and act. 'Orson, what shall we do about Mr Lewis? We can't just leave his body in the barn.'

'I guess we'd better bury him here.' Peel looked at Greeley. 'We have a small area set aside as a graveyard. It already holds the graves of two cowboys who came to grief last year. Pretty little spot.'

'Ruth might not like that. She might want to take him home so he can be buried close by her and she can visit his grave every day.'

'I know, Betsy, but heaven knows how long it'll be before she's able to travel to her farm because heaven knows how long it'll be before Wells Fargo can run a stage through here again. And we have nowhere to keep him in the meantime.'

'Can't one of the men take Ruth and the body home in the buckboard?'

'I don't think so, sweetheart. Not yet anyway. The conditions are still bad out there and to drive the buckboard down the hills might be to risk a spill. You don't want any of the men to risk their lives, do you?'

'Certainly not!'

'I don't see any alternative. So we might as well hold the service this afternoon after we've given her the chance to say goodbye to him.'

'At least we can give her our support. She keeps telling me what a good man and a good husband Clarence was

134

and how she doesn't know what she'll do without him.'

'She didn't even want to be on that stage,' Greeley said. 'She wanted to stay in Talbot till the storm blew over. Even worse he was killed for nothing.'

'And, Betsy, tell her we'll find a way to get her home as soon as we can so she can be with her son. She mustn't think we're just going to let her get on with it by herself.'

CHAPTER TWENTY-TWO

The other hands returned with Bill Brown and the horses before Greeley and Williams left for Serenity. The coach driver was no worse for his ordeal of being out by himself, all night in the cold. He said he had spent the time cuddling up to the horses and they'd kept him warm. He went to sit by Daniels' bed where both men were fussed over by Betsy Peel.

The men had brought back the luggage from the stage. Greeley was pleased to be reunited with his saddlebags and rifle.

Shortly afterwards he said goodbye to the Peels. He didn't feel up to the long ride he had in front of him, but at the same time he knew he couldn't delay any longer. 'Thank you for all your help. I'm sorry I brought trouble to your door.'

'It wasn't your fault,' Betsy said kissing his cheek. 'I surely hope that you catch up with that wicked girl. Sal the Gal what a ridiculous name! She deserves to be punished for the misery she's caused. Mr Greeley, promise me you'll do your best to make things right.'

'I will.'

Greeley and Williams didn't speak much as they rode down through the hills. While the safest route was to keep to the stagecoach road, Peel had suggested, and his foreman agreed, that the quickest and shortest way by far was to cut across country. The trail might be dangerous after all the rain, but then the stagecoach road could be just as bad, especially as lower down it criss-crossed the river several times. And once they came out of the hills it would then be a straight and reasonably short ride across the valley to the river with Serenity on its other side.

For the most part the two men had to ride single-file along a narrow, winding trail where trees pressed close, making it cold and gloomy. Deep canyons far below were marked by weird rock formations. They were forced to back-track a couple of times when the trail became impass-able, with fallen trees and rocks. Once a lengthy detour was necessary. But luckily for the most part the way remained clear of any obstructions and while the ground was soaked through, they met with no real flooding.

It was early evening, the shadows lengthening all round them, when they reached the valley floor. They were almost there.

Greeley came to a halt, took a drink from his canteen and handed it to Williams, who said, 'How you feeling?'

'My head aches. Badly. I'm not sure I can go on much longer.'

'It ain't too far now.'

137

'Thank God for that. We haven't seen any sign of Norton and Sal.'

'Which could mean they're a good way ahead of us or they stuck to the road. Or they don't know the area and they're riding round in circles. Make it easier to catch 'em if so.'

Somehow Greeley doubted Sal was the type to ride round in circles. She would know where she wanted to go and how to get there.

After visiting several of the farms closest to Serenity, Marshal Rayner reached the river just as evening was settling in. Although warned by Evans as to what to expect, seeing it for himself was a shock. He could hardly believe the devastation. The bridge had almost completely disappeared. And the water was full of branches and bushes tumbling over and over in the current. Even so, to his experienced eyes, it appeared the water was beginning to go down slightly and thankfully the banks had held.

But Frank was also right in that it was no use trying to rebuild the bridge just yet. Serenity would have to remain cut off from Talbot for a few days more at least.

He was about to turn back when movement on the far side of the river caught his eye. He stopped and stared.

Two riders were approaching the spot where the bridge should be. He recognized one as the foreman at the OP Ranch, although he didn't know his name. The second was a stranger. As he watched, they came to a halt, clearly not knowing what to do.

Raising himself in the stirrups, he yelled and waved his hat in the air. Finally he attracted their attention and pointed downriver. A mile or so lower down, the river widened out and there, hopefully, the water would be shallower and slower, making it possible for them to ride across.

When he got there he saw he was right. The stagecoach would find it difficult to get across without the risk of being overturned, but the horse-riders should manage it. He could actually see the riverbed at the edges.

Greeley and Williams reached the other side of the bank a couple of minutes later.

'Looks OK,' Williams said. 'We ain't had a wasted journey.'

Greeley said nothing. After what had happened at the ford, he was reluctant to ride into the river. Worse, he was now feeling terrible from where Sal had slugged him, his head throbbing so abominably he could hardly see for the pain. He was shivering. He wasn't sure whether he'd be able to handle the horse. Still, he couldn't stay where he was.

Letting Williams lead the way, he urged his animal down the bank and into the river. The horse strained against the force of the water and began to swim for the opposite shore with Greeley clinging to the saddle. At one point a sudden surge in the tide had him fearing they would both go under. Then the horse recovered and found its footing and soon it was struggling out the other side.

He was on dry land again, feeling sick and swaying slightly in the saddle. He was glad when Williams rode up to him and reached across to steady him.

'Who's this?' Rayner asked the foreman.

'Gustavus Greeley.'

'What, the bounty hunter?' That was a surprise. Rayner had thought him another cowboy from the OP. 'Well, you sure look as if you've been in the wars.'

The bump on Greeley's head was large and red. His eyes were blurred and there were purpling bruises on the side of his face. 'I have.'

'What the hell is going on? What's been happening? Where's Norton?'

'It's a long story,' said Williams.

'Then let's go back to Serenity and you can tell me all about it when we get there.'

It wasn't long before Greeley found himself being treated by Doctor O'Connor, although he couldn't remember much about getting to his surgery; his head was thumping fit to burst and he could hardly see through the pain. But after the doctor bathed the wound, rubbed some salve into it and put him to bed, he began to feel slightly better.

Williams, having received the doctor's agreement to go back with him to the OP in the morning, had taken himself off to one of the saloons.

It was quiet in the room, the lamp turned down low and Greeley, feeling warm and comfortable for the first time in a long while, quickly told Marshal Rayner and his deputy everything that had taken place from the time he'd caught the stagecoach to now.

When he finished, Rayner shook his head. 'Well, while I am surprised at Sal the Gal committing cold blooded murder, I can't say I'm surprised about the rest of it. You know, Frank, it might have crossed our minds she was on

140

her way to help Norton when she escaped from Madam Queenie's after stealing all her money.'

That was why Sal was so anxious about her carpetbag; it contained the stolen money.

'We knew she was a favourite of Norton's and that she could twist him round her little finger. To be honest, Gus, she was as much trouble as him, although in a different way of course.'

'Sal was a girl with big ideas,' Evans added. 'She always said she was going places and lately she wanted to go to them with Norton.'

'I ain't too sure he always felt the same way. He was the type to be after a good time, not a future. I pity him if Sal ever realizes that.'

'But you never put two and two together?' Greeley said.

'No,' Rayner admitted. 'It wouldn't've made much difference if we had. Shortly after Sal run off, the storm hit and there wasn't time or chance to go after her. We thought she'd got caught out in the open and was probably lying dead or badly injured somewhere.' He shook his head. 'Instead she turned herself into Sarah Fuller and made for Talbot. She was certainly taking a risk but it was the sort of foolhardy thing Sal would do.'

'She might have well gotten away with it were it not for the accident,' Evans added. 'Even Sal couldn't prevent that.'

Despite everything the girl had done, the two lawmen obviously held a grudging admiration for her.

'Something's puzzling me,' Greeley said. 'How did she know I'd caught Norton and was bringing him back here on the stage? Was it common knowledge?'

'Not until after Sal had gone. Then the news spread like wildfire. What is it, Charley?'

Rayner said, 'I wouldn't be surprised if Sal hadn't got to Greg Morgan. He's our telegraph operator,' he added for Greeley's benefit. 'Be just like the old fool to be taken in by Sal's promises so he'd do whatever she wanted.'

'And, Charley, if you remember, the night Sal ran off, Morgan was at Queenie's demanding entrance because he'd been promised a night of free loving. Naturally Queenie laughed in his face and he was promptly seen off the premises.' Evans laughed.

'When we heard we just thought he was drunk and acting stupid. Since then he's gone round with a long face and a surly ashamed-of-himself manner. Reckon he's in trouble at home too. More than usual that is. His wife don't stand any nonsense.' Rayner paused. 'I'll speak to him tomorrow and if we're right I'll have his job for him. Stupid idiot.'

'He's probably sorry now,' Evans said.

'Don't matter. He has a responsible position. It was his actions helped get Clarence Lewis killed.'

'Did you know Lewis?' Greeley asked, taking a sip of water from the glass the doctor had left on the table by the bed.

'Vaguely. The family live about three miles out of town. They come in now and then to stock up and sell their goods. Can't say I took to him much. He was a bit of a know-it-all and liked the sound of his own voice.'

'That was what got him into trouble.'

'But Mrs Lewis seems like a lovely lady, real pleasant, and their son has grown up into a fine young man,' Evans put in. 'He was friends with Arthur.'

'Well, Sal killed him for nothing. Mrs Lewis never let her husband go anywhere near the saloons and Lewis himself would never have gone into a brothel. You know, I reckon Queenie had a lucky escape.'

So had Greeley.

'Sal could easily have killed her too. I'll have to tell her. Stop her squawking and complaining. Norton had better watch out as well.' Rayner laughed. 'Now, Gus, I suggest you get some rest. You look whacked out.'

'I feel it.' Greeley could hardly keep his eyes open any longer. 'I'll head out in the morning after them.'

'Let's see how you feel first.'

Greeley was in no fit state to argue. Before his eyes closed he determined that, come what may, the next day he was riding out after Sal the Gal and Darren Norton.

CHAPTER
TWENTY-THREE

That night Norton and Sal lay in one another's arms beside a small campfire.

Sal had even managed to steal some food from the Peels so that they hadn't gone hungry. There was water in the two canteens. She was someone who always thought ahead and who always thought of everything.

'You really are a marvel,' Norton said, admiration tinged with a growing disquiet.

Now she sat up, gave Norton a quick kiss and sat with her knees drawn up and her arms around them, staring into the fire. 'Before I set out to rescue you, I thought about the best way to get to San Francisco,' she said.

'Are we going to make a run for the nearest railroad halt?'

'No.' She shook her head. 'That's what that fool Rayner will expect us to do. He'll either send men there after us or send a telegram to whoever is in charge. No, we'll do what's completely unexpected. We'll ride for Tucson.'

144

Norton frowned. 'But that's miles away.'

'Exactly,' Sal said. 'No one will ever suspect we'd go there. From Tucson we can catch a stagecoach into California and there change to a train. I know it'll be a much longer journey but that way we'll fool everyone and we won't get caught. They won't know where we've gone or how!'

'I suppose you're right.' It all sounded much too complicated to Norton. He just wanted to get as far away from Serenity and that damn bounty hunter and the prospect of hanging, as quickly as he could.

'Of course I am.' Sal allowed herself to bask in the glory of her own cleverness. 'When we reach San Francisco I'll start looking for some suitable premises to set up as a brothel.' She patted her bag containing the stolen money. 'A fancy one that's even better than Queenie's with swish red curtains, thick carpets and comfortable beds.' Her eyes took on a faraway look; she could picture it exactly. 'It doesn't have to be too large, not at first, although I expect to be able to expand in a few years time because San Francisco is full of sailors and prospectors and those searching for the end of the rainbow, and willing to spend a fortune to find it! Perfect.' They would all hurry to her place of business and she would take all their money; some gold too if she was lucky. 'Why we might even be able to buy a saloon or perhaps a gambling hall as well. With your skill at cards. . . .'

Norton sighed. In truth he really wasn't that good.

'. . . .We should make a success of that too. In the meantime you can help me run the brothel and kick out any troublemakers.'

145

Norton's heart was sinking further with each word. Usually he liked to hear Sal talk. She was always so full of ideas and dreams. They sounded like pie in the sky to someone like him, although he didn't doubt that she would succeed in doing what she'd set her mind on. It sounded wonderful – for her. What was not so wonderful was the fact that her plans included him.

He'd heard Sal's ideas on numerous occasions before. She'd often spoken of them when they'd been in bed together at Queenie's. But while he'd agreed to go along with her and become her business partner he'd done so simply because it was what she wanted to hear. In fact, he'd always meant to leave Serenity far behind before she could put those ideas into practice. He thought she'd understood that, understood he wasn't one for settling down, but clearly, being so caught up with what she wanted, she never thought someone else might not want the same and she hadn't understood at all. Never had he imagined that he'd be here in this position, beholden to her, on the run and heading for California and a life he most certainly didn't want.

Norton had never planned anything in his life. He was too busy doing whatever he liked to do at the time, enjoying himself, to ever think about his future. Except that that future most certainly didn't include knowing what he was expected to do, day in and day out, in the same place, forever more. He preferred moving on when he was bored with a town and its people. Doing nothing if he felt like it, lazing around all day, drinking or gambling.

This life with Sal meant going to a place of work and working!

Sal turned her head to look at him and said sharply, 'You're quiet, Darren. What's the matter?'

'Nothing.'

A note of steel came into her voice. 'I hope you ain't thinking of changing your mind about going into business with me.'

'No, of course not. Nothing like that, Sal.'

'Good. I wouldn't like that, not after everything I've risked and done for you.'

'You can count on me,' Norton smiled, doing his best to hide his ill-ease.

While Sal had always been determined to succeed, he knew now that she was also unpredictable and ruthless. He feared what she would do to him if she knew what was on his mind.

Norton decided that, while he admired her courage and singlemindedness, he didn't like her much. Actually he also decided he was afraid of her. He really didn't want to be shackled to her much longer and he made up his mind that sometime on the journey, when there was no danger to himself, he would run out on her and run far away where she had no chance of finding him.

He also considered taking her money with him – imagining all the drinks and girls he could enjoy with it – but he decided he couldn't do that. After all, she *had* rescued him from facing the hangman. He knew a little bit about her past and thought she deserved the future she longed for. Even more important, she might well come after him to get it back.

CHAPTER TWENTY-FOUR

It was late the next morning before Greeley finally woke up. He was annoyed he'd slept so long but he had to admit he felt better for it. His headache had gone, he no longer felt sick and, when he got out of bed, there was no dizziness.

As he was getting dressed, Marshal Rayner came in. He smiled. 'Awake at last! Feeling better?'

'Yeah, thanks. You should have woken me sooner.'

'Doc said best to let you sleep. He also said you must have something to eat and drink before we set out. Don't frown like that. It always does to obey the doctor! And don't worry. There's food ready for you and the horses are waiting at the livery saddled and bridled. Meanwhile Doc's ridden back to the Peel ranch with Toby Williams. And I've put the fear of the devil into Greg Morgan.'

'Are you going to get him the sack?'

'No, I've decided not to, much as he deserves it, as I have no certain proof of his guilt, except in my own mind and from the way he behaved when I challenged him. Instead I'm going to give a hint to his wife about my suspicions. That'll be an even worse punishment, believe me! She'll give him hell.' Rayner grinned. 'Breakfast is waiting in Doc's kitchen. Don't worry, Gus, you must be a reasonably good tracker. So is Frank. Myself, I reckon they'll ride for the nearest railroad station. We'll find 'em soon enough.'

It didn't work out quite that easily.

It was soon clear that Norton and Sal were not headed for the railroad.

'Which other way are they likely to go?' Greeley asked.

'Not back into the hills where there's still likely to be storm damage,' Rayner said. 'Only a fool would do that, and Sal knows what she's about. Otherwise,' he shrugged, 'they could be heading almost anywhere. Whichever direction they ride in, they'll come to somewhere eventually.'

'It depends on whether they want to catch a train or the stagecoach,' Evans pointed out. 'Or if they intend to ride all the way to California.'

'I doubt they'd do that,' Greeley said. 'It'd take far too long.'

He was starting to feel anxious. Norton and Sal had a good start on them and he was afraid they could lose them altogether. After all it wasn't even certain they still planned to go to San Francisco. Sal might have changed her mind and decided to head East to somewhere like Santa Fe or perhaps into Texas.

'We'll just have to scout around until we come across their trail,' Rayner said.

No one asked what they would do if they didn't find it.

'If we head back towards the hills, we might discover where they came out into the valley,' he added. 'We can track 'em from there.'

It was late afternoon with shadows stretching across the valley and it was beginning to look as if they wouldn't succeed, might even have to give up, when, at last, Evans, who was riding a little way distant from the other two, came across the tracks of two horses. He fired his gun as a signal for them to join him.

'It must be them,' Greeley said, dismounting to look at the tracks. 'Surely no one else has come down from the hills since the storm and these look fresh to me.'

Evans nodded in agreement. 'Day or two old is all.'

After following the tracks for some way, Rayner came to a halt, removed his Stetson and ran a hand through his hair. 'They're heading for Tucson.'

'You sure?' Greeley said in surprise. 'That's miles from here.'

'It's the nearest place in the direction they're going, Gus. Or rather the only place of any note. The hamlets along the way ain't up to much and ain't on the stage-line. Tucson is.'

'They could be trying to fool us into thinking they're going one way whereas they're actually going another,' Evans said.

Rayner shook his head. 'No reason for 'em to do that, Frank. They don't know we've got after them so quickly.'

Greeley agreed. 'No. I could still be at the Peel ranch and no one in Serenity knows what happened.'

'For once in her life, Sal's been too clever for her own

good,' Rayner said with a smile. 'If they'd gone for the railroad they'd be on a train by now. I doubt we'd've caught up with 'em in time. And while she had no way of knowing it, the telegraph is still down and I couldn't've sent out any messages about them. Tucson is a long way off and now we have the chance to catch up.'

Greeley nodded. He might have to ride all night to overtake them, but ride all night he would. And he knew Rayner and Evans would follow him.

'There they are!'

The cry went up from Greeley as the small posse crested the ridge of the rocky slope. They had, indeed, ridden for most of the night, only stopping now and then to rest the horses. Once for a long rest for themselves because, as Rayner said, it wouldn't do to go without some sleep. They had to keep fresh and alert.

During the night they'd found the remains of an old campfire.

'Norton and Sal, it must be,' Greeley said after a quick inspection. 'They stopped for quite a while by the looks of things. They'll probably have made camp tonight as well. They do, we should catch them up before too long.'

He was right. For now their quarry was in their sights.

The two riders were on the far side of a small rock-strewn valley. They had crossed a creek, whose waters were much higher than normal, and were heading into the next line of hills.

'Let's get 'em!' Evans cried. He dug his spurs into his horse's sides and with a startled neigh it set off at the charge.

Greeley swore to himself. He'd have preferred to sound a note of caution. Tried to get closer before they were spotted. Made sure of the capture. Too late for that. Evans was already galloping down the hillside with Rayner in close pursuit. It was only a matter of moments before Norton and Sal realized they'd been found.

CHAPTER TWENTY-FIVE

Norton looked back over his shoulder. 'Hell!' He swore long and loudly. 'Look!'

Three riders. Galloping fast towards them. Already splashing across the creek. Close enough for him to recognize Greeley and Marshal Rayner.

'How did they find us?' Sal screamed in frustration. Damn! Damn! Damn! Could they outrun them? Probably best not to try. Their horses were tired and the terrain was rough. They might be overtaken or shot. Anyway she had spotted a high pile of misshapen boulders in the near distance. She pointed them out to Norton. 'We'll make a stand there.' Settle the matter once and for all.

'Quick!' Greeley yelled, seeing what Norton and Sal were about.

'We won't get there in time to stop them reaching the rocks.' Rayner pulled his rifle from the scabbard and fired once. It was a futile gesture. He was too far away to hit anything.

Norton and Sal dismounted and hunkered down behind the rocks.

Sal smiled. It was a good spot. The hill their pursuers had to climb towards them provided little or no cover; they would be easy targets.

'Let them get close,' she said. 'Then we can pick them off.'

The posse had reached the bottom of the hill when the first shot rang out.

The bullet slammed into the ground right in front of Evans's horse. It reared in fright, causing an equally startled deputy to fall off. He hit the ground with a thud and the animal shied away from him.

'Get off your horse!' Rayner shouted to Greeley. Mounted, they were vulnerable. On foot it would be easier to dodge behind rocks and keep out of the way of any gunfire. 'Frank, you OK?'

The young man was sitting up, holding a hand to his head. 'I think so.'

But his hand came away covered with blood and from the dazed look on his face it didn't seem he would be taking any further part in the chase.

'Stay put and keep the horses safe.' It would be no use to lose the animals out in the middle of nowhere as they were. 'Gus, come with me. Stay low.'

Greeley didn't need to be warned. As they scrambled up the steep, shale-covered hill, more shots sounded, striking chips off the rocks near them.

He paused to take a quick look round. From where they

were it was no point firing back. There were no targets to aim at. And it would be too risky to try rushing Norton and Sal. Then he spotted a plateau to their left. 'Charley, look. We get over there we should have a good view of their hiding place and hopefully be shielded a little by the small overhang.'

Carefully they began to edge their way over towards it.

Seeing them and realizing that if Greeley and Rayner made it they could get clear shots at them, Norton fired off several bullets in their direction. None hit either man. 'Damn that bounty hunter. There's no stopping him. And I'm almost out of bullets.'

'So am I. Oh, Darren, I'm sorry.' Sal bent to kiss him. 'We've still got a chance to make a run for it. They're on foot and will have to go back for their horses. That'll give us a head start.'

Norton knew her optimism was misplaced. They couldn't run forever. He didn't want to be forever looking over his shoulder. Greeley would never give up coming after him. Not now. Not when his pride in his job was at stake. As well as $100 bounty.

For a moment he wondered what to do. Surrender? No way. Make a fight of it with Sal and risk getting her killed? No, he couldn't do that. So, for the first time in his life he decided to put someone else first. Try to give Sal the chance she deserved. Because, despite everything she'd done, Greeley might be satisfied with just Norton and the reward.

Besides he was a gambler and this, his greatest gamble, might just, with luck, pay off.

'You go on without me, Sal. Get to San Francisco.'

'No, I'm not leaving you,' she said, making him feel guilty for the way earlier he'd been intending to walk out on her.

'Sorry, Sal, I ain't going to California with you. I hope you have the life you want. I love you.'

He stood up.

'Darren! What are you doing? Get down.'

Taking no notice, he stepped forward and began to fire his gun.

Greeley pushed Rayner out of the way and dropped to the ground. Peering round a boulder, he shouted across at the young man, 'Darren, give up! You don't have to do this.' But he knew he wouldn't. And he didn't.

Norton fired again. The bullet came precariously close, whizzing past Greeley's ear with a horrible whine. The next shot might hit either him or the lawman.

Cursing, Greeley steadied himself. He raised his rifle, aiming carefully. Another shot from Norton. Even closer. He was left with no choice.

He pulled the trigger. He didn't miss.

Norton let out a cry. Dropping the gun he fell forward. He lay still.

As Greeley got to his feet, Rayner shouted out a warning, 'Sal's still there. Be careful.'

But there were no more shots.

Was she already dead? Or just biding her time?

'Cover me.' Greeley started to zig-zag up the slope. Nothing. He reached the spot where Norton lay on his stomach. The young man was clearly dead. Greeley's bullet had taken him in the chest close to his heart. He glanced round. The two horses were tethered a little way off. Of Sal there was no sign.

Then he spotted her. She was standing on top of a huge boulder looking down . . . at what? She was still holding the carpetbag which was so precious to her.

Hearing his approach, she turned to look at him. He paused, holding out his hands towards her, not wanting her to do anything that would force him to shoot her. 'Sal, Sarah . . .' he began.

She smiled at him.

And jumped.

'No!' Greeley yelled in horror.

He ran towards where she'd been. When he got there, he realized she'd been staring at the creek, which was a ribbon of blue far, far below.

He could see no sign of her body. Neither smashed on the rocks on the way down nor drowned in the water.

She had disappeared.

CHAPTER TWENTY-SIX

'You don't think Sal got away, do you?' Orson Peel asked while Betsy looked anxiously on.

Greeley shrugged. 'Me and Rayner searched the hillside and the creek for the rest of the day. We never found a trace of her. But,' he spread his hands, 'I really can't see how she could have survived a fall like that. It was a long way down, there were rocks all round and the creek was deep and swift.'

'But . . .' Betsy began.

'No, Mrs Peel, she must be dead.'

'Then why didn't you find her?'

'The water probably took her body downstream a fair way to where it'll be lost forever.'

Although if anyone could have survived, Greeley supposed it might be Sal the Gal. And even if they hadn't recovered her body, there was also the question of the carpetbag. There had been no sign of that either.

'At least Norton got his comeuppance,' Peel said.

'Yeah, but Rayner and Evans would've preferred to have taken him back alive to Serenity so he could stand trial. This way he's cheated the hangman.' Greeley still got his $100 though.

It was a few days after the chase across the valley. He had returned with a buckboard to the Peel ranch to see how Peel and Daniels were faring and to accompany Mrs Lewis back to her farm and her son.

Betsy Peel poured him out another cup of coffee. 'She's just about ready to leave,' she said. 'I'm grateful to you, Mr Greeley, for the offer to escort her home. It saves any of us having to do so while there's still so many things left to repair, although we would have been willing of course.'

Daniels had also recovered sufficiently to be ready to go with them.

And Wells Fargo had sent men out to recover the stage-coach, although no one knew when the route would re-open for business. Bill Brown had gone along to help. So had a dispirited Harry Anderson, who didn't know what he was going to do with no money, no horse and no goods to sell.

'It's the least I can do,' Greeley said.

'You weren't at fault,' Peel said as his wife nodded. 'Not at all.'

It didn't matter how many times people told him that, Greeley still felt guilty over what had happened and always would.

Even so, despite all that Sal the Gal had done, he couldn't help but harbour a small, lingering hope that maybe, just maybe, hard though it was to believe, the girl was still, somehow, alive. She had been callous and heartless, only thinking of herself, but at the same time she'd certainly had pluck. Not many girls would have done what she had; not many men either.

Knowing the Peels wouldn't appreciate such a sentiment, he didn't say so.

Two months later Marshal Rayner sent Greeley a cutting from a San Francisco newspaper. Rayner had scrawled one word across the top 'Sal' following by several question marks.

The headline stated in bold black letters: 'Madam Sara's is now open for business'.

Greeley read: 'San Francisco's newest and fanciest bawdy house got off to a flying start last night. Men flocked to its doors, despite suspecting they were going to be overcharged, lured by the promise that the whiskey would be good, not watered down rotgut, and the girls would go that extra mile to please. The fact that Sara herself is a pretty young woman with poise and dash helped too. We have no hesitation in saying the place is sure be a riproaring success.'

He couldn't help smiling.

Perhaps one day he'd make the trip to San Francisco and find out if Madam Sara was indeed Sal the Gal. And, if so, whether sometimes she might remember a time when she went by a different name and when she wanted a future with a handsome lover.

Meanwhile it was obvious Rayner was not going to do anything except let her enjoy her success and thus so would Greeley.